Not a Game

CARDENO C.

Perfect Imperfections: Wow…reading something sexy is great…hearing it in your ear…PRICELESS!! I was hooked from the very first moment I started this book until the very last word. I enjoyed this book as there wasn't tons of angst or drama. It was simply a sweet, lovely romance about two men falling in love and that made it so much more sweeter.

—*Love Bytes Reviews*

Strange Bedfellows: This is a fun beautifully written book of two men meeting at a time in their life that they are receptive to finding love. A book about finding yourself and becoming the man you are meant to be. About love and devotion.

—*Night Owl Reviews*

The Half of Us: When you want the meaning of true family and love this is the book to pick up in either ebook or audio form it is an great read.

—*Redz World*

Strong Enough: Strong Enough is a sweet and sexy read that will leave you with a smile on your face. Strong Enough is a very easy book to recommend and I know once you read this gem of a story you'll want to read more books written by this amazing author.

—*Top2Bottom Reviews*

Walk With Me: This book has everything you could ask for in a romance and then some. I could not recommend a better read if you are looking for something with a genuine, romantic feel.

—*Guilty Indulgence Book Club*

Just What the Truth Is: I loved this book! C. Cardeno kept me frustrated with Ben, laughing with him and sometimes sobbing right along with him on his journey to self awareness and a life worth living in every respect. C. Cardeno's characterizations and spot on dialog were so wonderfully executed that the story zipped along and I was finishing the end before I knew it.

—*Scattered Thoughts and Rogue Words*

An accidental meeting and a misunderstanding lead to a life-altering connection.

A new job, a new city, and hopefully a new life. When chubby gamer Oliver Barnaby receives a job offer from the best boutique game developer in the country, he leaves his family and his less than spectacular existence in Oklahoma without a second's hesitation. Determined to change more than his career and his geography, Oliver implements a plan to finally land a boyfriend. Step one is improving his skills in the bedroom.

A life that looks perfect on paper, but feels empty in reality. Attractive, successful, charismatic Jaime Snow has a life other people envy. His already booming business is growing. He isn't lacking in friends. And he has no trouble finding a date. But there's an emptiness in Jaime's heart and a hole in his life that only the right man can fill.

An accidental meeting, a misunderstanding, and falling in love. When Oliver and Jaime end up at the same bar at the same time, they each see something they want in the other. Going to bed together that first night is easy. Building the lifetime relationship they both desperately crave will require trust, time, and a little misunderstanding.

Word count: 55,872

Dedication

To Tamra Johnson with appreciation for your kind words and support of my writing.

To Shee Reader with gratitude for your friendship and uplifting demeanor.

To Jaime Chan with thanks for your excellent character naming skills.

And to the people fighting for social justice: Thank you.

Chapter 1

H E HAD CHOSEN the bar because of its name: The Bookstore. It was clever and unusual and he had laughed internally at how happy his mother would be if he told her he was spending time at the Bookstore instead of in front of his computer. Oliver's entire life, she had mourned the fact he wasn't a reader, and even though he had now moved two thousand miles away from their home in Oklahoma City, she still sent him books she was sure he'd love. Maybe someday he'd open one of them.

For now, he glanced down at the only book he had read countless times and adjusted it at the edge of his table to make the spine as visible as possible. The title—*Coding*—wasn't as clever as the bar name, but the information and the way it was phrased had clicked perfectly in Oliver's brain when he was a college freshman. He had long since moved past the information inside, but the textbook was the closest thing he had to a security blanket, so he had held onto it through four years of progressively more complicated computer science classes, three dead-end computer repair and technical support jobs, and a move to Seattle to finally, *finally*, live his dream developing video games. When he had to pick a way to identify himself to the stranger who would guide him on the last phase of his journey toward living the life he had always wanted, the first thing that came to Oliver's mind was the book that had started it all.

With the spine facing the bar and walkway and his glass empty, Oliver had nothing left to do but wait or get his phone out to play a quick turn on *Clash of Clans*. He reached into his pocket almost before his brain had formulated the thought. A quick glance at his screen confirmed it was still twenty minutes shy of eight o'clock. Oliver prided himself on timeliness, something his father had drummed into him since he was a boy, and after two months in Seattle, he hadn't yet gotten a handle on how long it took to get anywhere, so he had erred on the side of caution and ended up arriving half an hour early.

In his head, his mother lectured him about playing on his phone when he should be paying attention to people, but he was twenty-eight years old, and she was too far away to see him, so he ignored her and tried to lose himself in a game. Besides, taking his mind off why he was in that bar would stop him from falling headfirst into an anxiety attack, and even his mother would agree that was a good thing in a social setting. Not that she would ever have the chance to know about his plans that evening, because, despite how close they were, this was one activity Oliver absolutely would not share with his family. Or anyone else for that matter.

Nerves rising, he scratched his upper back through his shirt with one hand and his thigh with the other. Recognizing what he was doing, he forced his hands away before he broke the skin. Hoping for a distraction, he jerked his gaze toward his pop when, suddenly, from the corner of his eye, he noticed someone moving in his direction. Instinctively, Oliver grabbed the glass and scrunched over it, using the act of sipping from a straw as a shield to keep himself from staring at people who inevitably didn't notice him. But when the man didn't veer away and instead came closer, Oliver glanced up and realized the stranger was looking right at his book. Which meant he was either coming to tease the chubby nerd for having a textbook at a bar on a Friday night or…

Oh my God. This is him. Oliver kept his head down but couldn't stop himself from flicking his gaze back and forth between his still empty glass and the approaching man.

Older than Oliver, but not too old, broad shoulders, light eyes, short dark hair, and a sculpted face. The man stopped right next to the table, waited for Oliver to look up, and then said, "Interesting reading choice." He tapped the top of the cover and tried to meet Oliver's gaze.

Even though this was one situation where Oliver couldn't be rejected or laughed at, he still struggled to speak to such a handsome man, and he definitely couldn't make eye contact with him. And now that he was close enough for Oliver to see him clearly, he definitely knew that was true. He set his gaze on the man's chin and took in his features.

The dark hair was brown but it had strands of chestnut at the top and flecks of silver in the sideburns, which extended to the bottom of his earlobe. The light eyes were green, a pale shade that still managed to look warm. And the broad shoulders topped a chest so muscular that it stretched the black T-shirt he wore underneath a well-fitted jacket. This guy was fantasy material, and Oliver couldn't believe he had gotten so lucky.

"Is this book yours?"

"Yes," Oliver said hoarsely and then cleared his throat. "It's mine."

The man's forehead crinkled. He tilted his head to the side and stared at Oliver.

At first, the odd look discomforted him, but then Oliver remembered the social etiquette classes he had been forced to attend in middle school, and he realized where he had gone wrong.

"Please have a seat," he said, raising his hand toward the empty chair across from him. Though his voice still shook more than he would have liked, it was a bolder invitation than he usually gave. Of course, *usually* men didn't approach him, especially incredibly handsome men, and *usually* people didn't want to hang out with him, and *usually* he didn't look up escort services and set up a meeting. So today was anything but Oliver's usual.

"Thanks." The man pulled back the empty chair, sat, and then scooted it forward. "I'm Jaime." He reached his hand out.

Oliver glanced down at the hand, blinked, and then remembered his manners. "I'm Oliver." He wiped his sweaty palm on his jeans, took Jaime's hand, and shook it. "Oliver Barnaby."

Oh crap. Was giving his last name in this situation a bad idea? Oh well. If everything went as expected, Oliver would be spending time alone with this man, which would put him at more risk than sharing his name. He had made reservations at the hotel upstairs, which was expensive and not completely secure, but it had to be safer than bringing a stranger to his apartment.

"So, Oliver Barnaby." Grinning, Jaime glanced at the book and arched his eyebrows. "What are you doing here with this?"

Straight to the point. In Jaime's line of work, being direct made sense, but Oliver wasn't skilled at holding an articulate conversation with a live human so he fidgeted in his seat. "Well, uh…" He gulped.

"Late night study session?" The comment was teasing, but the tone held no malice and Jaime's expression, while most definitely amused, wasn't cruel.

4

"Sorry. I'm being silly." Oliver shook his head. "We both know why we're here so—" He drew in a deep breath. "I'm not sure how much he told you." He frowned and thought back to the brief phone call he'd had with the man from the ad. "Actually, I don't remember how much detail I gave him other than saying I needed someone experienced."

"Experienced?"

"Uh-huh. Because, uh." He looked at Jaime's handsome face and once again lost the power of speech.

He hadn't thought through how the escort agency would interpret his request but now he realized they had taken it to mean Oliver wanted someone a bit older. As luck would have it, older men were very much Oliver's type. Or they would be if he had a type. Someone probably needed to go on actual dates rather than just fantasize about them before he could say he had a type.

"Oliver?"

Oliver blinked.

"You were saying you needed someone experienced?"

"Right." He bobbed his head. "See the thing is, I didn't hire you for sex."

There was no missing the shock that crossed Jaime's face.

"That didn't come out right." Oliver quickly backtracked. The last thing he wanted was for Jaime to think he was being stiffed because then he'd get up and walk out and Oliver would have to start his search all over again. The odds of finding someone as attractive and nice as Jaime to teach him were so low they rounded to zero. "I know what escort means and I'm all set to pay you. I have the money." He patted his pocket and said an internal thank-you for his new company's generosity. "What I meant was that I don't want to have sex with you."

Jaime chuckled and arched his eyebrows, but he didn't say anything.

"Ugh." Oliver shook his head. "I didn't mean that either." He raised his hand and moved it up and down in Jaime's direction. "Look at you. Obviously, I want to have sex with you. But it's not about eating the meal, it's about learning to fish, you know?"

"I think I'm getting the picture, but why don't you fill in the details?" Jaime lowered his voice. "And try to keep the whole paying for sex thing out of it." One side of his lips rose in a crooked smile. "We are in public after all and not *everything* is legal in Washington."

Oh God. Oliver jerked his head from side to side, checking to see if anyone was close enough to hear him. The bar wasn't big and there were a decent number of customers, so someone probably had. He leaned forward, his belly squishing against the table. "Do you think people will call the police? Should we leave?"

"No and"—Jaime's smile shifted from amused to wicked— "eventually. But first, tell me about learning to fish." Jaime settled into his chair and crossed his arms over his chest, his biceps giving the gray suede jacket a workout. "I assume we aren't talking about the great outdoors, so what exactly are you hiring me to teach you?"

When he had come up with the idea to hire an escort, Oliver had focused on how much it would cost, where to do it, and what he'd be able to squeeze into one night. He had also spent a decent amount of time second-guessing his plan. But he had never considered how he would explain what he wanted to the man he paid to help him.

"Do you guys have like, uh, confidentiality requirements?"

Oliver asked.

Jaime arched his eyebrows. "Confidentiality?"

"Yeah." Oliver bobbed his head. "What I tell you has to stay between us, right?"

"Well." Jaime's mouth turned up at the corners and then he licked his lips, coughed, and said, "I'm not a psychiatrist or an attorney, so there's not a licensing board out there keeping me honest, but I'll give you my word to keep this just between us. How's that?"

After considering the response and his alternatives for a couple of seconds, Oliver said, "That works."

"Glad we got the preliminaries out of the way." Jaime smiled. "Tell me what you need, Oliver."

When he said Oliver's name, Jaime's voice dropped, going deeper and raspier. The tone sent a pang through Oliver's gut and reminded him why this man got paid to do what he did. That made what Oliver had to say even more humiliating, but he didn't want his life in Seattle to be like his life in Oklahoma, so he pushed through the shame and forced himself to speak.

"I'm pretty sure I'm bad in bed and I want help with that." He bit his lip. "Real help. Not what people brag about online." He had read endless blogs and subscribed to chat rooms, but loath as he was to admit it, the internet didn't have all the answers.

Looking surprised, Jaime blinked a few times, cleared his throat, and then said, "Why do you think you're bad in bed?"

That question was easy to answer. "My ex told me."

The good-natured, amused expression disappeared from Jaime's face. "Your ex sounds like a dick. Find someone else and forget about him."

"That's just it. I can't find someone else." Realizing he

sounded whiney, Oliver took a moment to breathe. He sat up straight, rolled his neck, and then ruined his attempt at looking confident by slumping. "People never like me in real life. I'm twenty-eight and Ted was the only guy who's ever been willing to sleep with me. That was four years ago." His voice shook. "I need help."

"Hey." Jaime's eyes softened, and he leaned forward, curling his hand around Oliver's forearm. "It's going to be okay. I promise."

Jaime's touch was ten times more potent than his voice, and suddenly, Oliver wanted to follow through on his plans for the night because of something entirely unrelated to learning and improving himself. He stayed perfectly still, letting the pleasurable feelings wash over him until Jaime removed his hand. And then the floodgates opened.

"I just moved to Seattle in August. Did I tell you that already? I want things to be different here. I got this great job making lots of money, and I have my own apartment, but that's not enough. I'm going to join a gym so I can lose weight, because I know guys aren't going to be interested in me like this." He waved his hand up and down beside his too fat, too flabby body. "I'll never be good-looking like you, but hopefully exercise will help, and I can diet too and then maybe someone will be interested, but then what? At some point we'll end up in bed and then he'll never want to see me again." He took a deep breath, his heart racing. "That's why I hired you. I need to get better, so if I actually find someone who's interested, I can hold on to him." He squeezed and released his hands and stared at Jaime, hoping he'd understand.

"All right," Jaime said calmly. "I hear you and I'm not turning you down." He looked at Oliver meaningfully, only continuing after Oliver nodded in understanding. "We can get out of here and do this, but before we do, I want you to know that not every guy is into gym bunnies or twinks. You're really good-looking, Oliver."

"You're getting paid to say that," Oliver mumbled, dropping his gaze from Jaime's eyes. Even that part of him was attractive—layers of green far more interesting than Oliver's own boring brown.

"No, I'm not." Jaime's jaw ticced as he spoke, and he sounded so firm that Oliver would have believed him if he hadn't found the man through an escort ad.

"It's fine," Oliver said. "I'm past worrying about being pathetic for paying for sex." He sighed and dragged his fingers through his hair, hoping he wasn't making the too long strands stick out in weird directions. "Actually, it helps. I'd never have the nerve to talk to a guy like you in real life, even if it was just to answer a question about directions or something." He rolled his eyes at his own shortcomings. "Knowing you can't laugh at me or judge me or turn me down makes this better." It made it possible. "That's all I need. Don't worry about the fake compliments."

"It wasn't fake."

Of course it was. Oliver was good-looking in the same way the bar was a bookstore. But that didn't matter and Jaime sounded angry, so Oliver stopped arguing and refocused the conversation on the reason they were both in the Bookstore that wasn't actually a bookstore. "I reserved a room upstairs in the hotel."

Jaime pulled his eyebrows together and narrowed his eyes and, for a horrible moment, Oliver was sure he had changed his mind and he was about to leave. Oliver was about to plead for another chance, but then Jaime's face smoothed and he rose from his chair.

"Lead the way, Oliver. I'm looking forward to"—he dragged his gaze over Oliver's body, his expression unlike any Oliver previously had seen directed at him—"fishing with you."

Chapter 2

HANDS CLUTCHING HIS coding textbook slash security blanket and head bowed, Oliver flicked his gaze to his right and stole glances at the man walking beside him. At six two in height and a weight that neared the three-hundred-pound mark, Oliver was used to being bigger than most people. But Jaime was a bit taller, and even though his muscular frame was considerably leaner, his wide shoulders, confident stride, and deep voice gave him a large presence.

Jaime looked like a man who could have or do anything, and for the next three hours, Oliver had him all to himself. He trembled from the thought of what that meant.

"Are you cold?" Jaime asked as they stepped into the elevator. He stood close enough for their shoulders to rub together.

"No." Oliver shook his head. "I have twenty-eight Oklahoma winters under my belt. Fall in Seattle is mild."

"You were shivering."

There was no judgment in Jaime's tone, but Oliver's cheeks warmed anyway. He dipped his chin and focused on the floor. "It was, uh, raining when I got to the bar and I walked a few blocks so I'm still a little damp." And a lot excited.

"We'll get you out of those wet clothes soon."

Oliver jerked his gaze to the side and stared at Jaime.

"What?" Jaime's expression was too innocent to be sincere. "Fishing isn't as productive with clothes on."

People didn't flirt with Oliver so it took him a second to realize it was happening and then, before his brain kicked in to stop him, he flirted right back. "I've seen some clips online that tell a different story."

Chuckling, Jaime said, "Yeah, so have I." He bumped his shoulder against Oliver's and grinned. "You want to tell me which types of clips you enjoy the most?"

The elevator dinged and they both stepped into the fourth floor hallway.

"Um, I…" Oliver's cheek temperature rose a few more degrees. "I don't…" He coughed.

"I'm making you uncomfortable."

It wasn't a question but Oliver answered anyway. "No."

"No?" Jaime arched his eyebrows, his tone disbelieving.

Shaking his head, Oliver said, "I'm actually way more comfortable with you than I normally am around strangers in real life." The words were out before Oliver could think about how ridiculous they'd sound and censor himself.

Thankfully, Jaime understood him. Without skipping a beat, he said, "As opposed to online?"

"Yeah." It wasn't a hard guess considering Oliver's appearance, which spoke for itself. Portly, pale, boring brown hair with a boring haircut. He looked like exactly who he was—a guy who spent his life behind a computer screen.

"I'm glad you're comfortable with me."

"It's easy when I know what someone expects from me and it's something I can deliver." Oliver shrugged, tucked his book under his arm, and got the keycard out of his pocket. "Usually, I don't understand what people want me to say or do or, even if I know how they want me to be, it's not who I am, so I end up making everyone uncomfortable or confused or bored out of their minds. With you, I know I'm supposed to pay a hundred bucks an hour, there's a two-hour minimum, and condoms are required. If I stick to those requirements, everyone's satisfied. I can do that, no problem, so it's all good." He pushed the door open, stepped inside, and then turned around to see Jaime quietly standing in the hallway, showing no indication of movement. "Was that… I hope I didn't insult you," Oliver said, worrying his word choice, though accurate, had been too crass.

Shaking his head, Jaime put his palm on the door to keep it open, stepped into the room, and then let the door swing shut. "Simple, straightforward guidelines mean a low risk of failing to meet expectations. I understand what you're saying."

"Exactly." Oliver let out a deep breath, relieved he hadn't offended Jaime, and not just because he didn't want to go through the effort of finding a different escort. The truth was, even though he probably had nothing in common with an incredibly handsome guy about ten years his senior who took money for sex, Oliver found himself liking Jaime.

"So," Jaime said, walking forward until his chest connected with Oliver's.

Oliver stepped backward into the room.

"Back to my question." Jaime followed, not leaving any distance between them. His eyes heated and his voice dropped lower, huskier. "What specifically do you want to do tonight?"

"I…" Oliver's breathing quickened. "I guess I don't know." Up until that moment, he had primarily focused on the takeaways from his encounter—gaining new skills that would make him more appealing to men and, hopefully, help him finally find a boyfriend. But with Jaime so close, Oliver's body reacted naturally, and all he could think about was *how* he would gain those skills. "What do guys usually like? Let's work on that."

His eyes twinkling and lips turning up in a smile, Jaime said, "You're sweet. And more innocent than most people I know."

Sweet and innocent were not in and of themselves bad things, and Jaime's fond expression implied that he hadn't meant them as insults, so Oliver wasn't offended. But he didn't necessarily agree with the assessment. Dropping his gaze, he tugged on a loose string in his jacket and said, "It's probably more that I'm inexperienced than anything else."

Nodding, Jaime trailed his fingertip over Oliver's hand, up his arm, to his collar. He looked Oliver in the eyes, traced the perimeter of his ear, and then stepped back and glanced around the room. "This is nice." He slipped his jacket off, tossed it on the dark leather chair in the corner of the room, and stepped over to the window. "View's not bad either." He toed off his shoes and turned around, his hands on his belt. Before Oliver could mentally catch up, Jaime's belt hung open and his jeans were unzipped. "The bed looks comfortable."

Not budging from his post at the edge of the room, Oliver flicked his gaze from Jaime to the bed. He hadn't yet responded when Jaime, dressed in his well-fitted black T-shirt, even better fitted gray boxer briefs, and a surprisingly colorful pair of socks, hopped onto the bed.

"So," Jaime said.

Oliver blinked.

"Tell me why you're inexperienced." He moved a few of the pillows around and then leaned back against them and crossed his arms over his chest and his legs at the ankles. "Were you brought up uber religious?"

Oliver was in a hotel room with a mostly undressed, somewhat older than average and very likely nicer than average underwear model who seemed genuinely interested in him. He would have thought he was dreaming but his imagination had never conjured a fantasy this good.

"Not religious, no." He shook his head and walked through the room and up to the bed. "The only times I remember being in a church were weddings and funerals."

"Come get in bed." Jaime patted the spot next to him. "It's comfy."

Going to bed with an experienced man was exactly what Oliver had planned for the night so the offer shouldn't have made him nervous. "Okay," he said, his voice trembling a smidge because, regardless of what he should be feeling, he was nervous. "I'll, uh, just take off my shoes."

"And your jacket."

Glancing down at his sleeves, Oliver confirmed that he still wore his coat. "Right. That too." He set his book next to the television and then slipped his jacket off and laid it beside Jaime's on the leather chair.

"And your pants."

Oliver jerked his gaze up.

"Maybe you sat on gum. You never know what can get on your pants when you're in a bar." Jaime grinned. "It'll be more sanitary this way."

"I hope you realize my underwear body looks nothing like your underwear body." Oliver sat on the ottoman and began untying his shoes.

"I'm looking forward to seeing your underwear body."

Saying Jaime was being paid to flatter him was pointless. They both knew why they were there. Besides, Oliver wanted to pretend the sincerity in Jaime's voice was real instead of a well-rehearsed line, so he finished removing his shoes, pulled off his plain white socks, and then rose and unfastened his pants. Once he had them on the chair next to his jacket, he made an executive decision and yanked his long-sleeved polo off, leaving himself in his white undershirt and blue checkered boxer shorts.

He took a deep breath and reminded himself that Jaime wouldn't gain anything by laughing at his client's overweight body and, based on their interaction so far, he was too nice a person to do that anyway. When Oliver stepped over to the bed and looked at Jaime again, he saw that he had been right to trust him—there was no mocking or derision in his expression. But it wasn't what was missing from Jaime's face that surprised Oliver, it was his look of appreciation as he slowly moved his gaze up and down Oliver's body. The man was either missing his calling as a gifted actor or he genuinely enjoyed what he saw.

"I saved you a spot." Jaime patted one of the pillows and arranged it beside him.

Despite his nervousness, Oliver chuckled. "Thanks." He walked to the empty side of the bed, climbed on, and settled beside Jaime.

"So," Jaime said.

"So?"

"You were telling me why you don't have a lot of experience."

"I guess I don't really know." Oliver shrugged. "Maybe it's because I've always been overweight or maybe it's because I don't look like guys in magazines or maybe it's because I'm boring." He sighed. "Whatever the reason, nothing has ever panned out. But now I can make a fresh start. I want Seattle me to be different than Oklahoma me. I have this great job now. I make enough to pay for my own place. I got a new car. But I'm not any closer to having a boyfriend."

Nodding slowly, Jaime said, "Usually people go on Grindr or

Scruff or hit a bar if they're looking for someone to date."

"I've tried all that. Back home and here too. It doesn't work." Oliver rolled his head from side to side, stretching his neck to work out the tension that accompanied his attempts to meet someone. Or, more accurately, his failures. "So when I saw the escort ads on *Backpage*, I figured it'd be a good place to start."

"When you tried the apps and the bars, did you talk to the guys like you have with me tonight?"

Oliver snorted.

"That's a no?" Jaime said, laughter in his voice.

"Every guy online wants to exchange pictures and even the ones who don't come right out and say 'no fatties' would block me if they saw my chest or my ass." He paused. "And if I wanted to send some random on the internet a picture of my dick, which I don't, I wouldn't be able to do it without my belly being in the shot." That comment reminded Oliver of something he had found amusing. "Did you know there are professional photographers who take dick pics?"

"Seriously?"

Nodding, Oliver said, "Uh-huh. Saw it online. They make them natural so people can send them like they're impromptu selfies, but really, they're staged with lights and angles and whatever else."

"You're not thinking of hiring a photographer for your dick, are you?" Jaime was clearly trying to keep his expression and tone neutral, but his acting skills had apparently reached their limit because he sounded slightly horrified.

"What if I said yes?" Oliver teased.

"Then I'd offer to take the pictures," Jaime replied without skipping a beat.

Taken off guard, Oliver's cheeks heated.

"Seriously though." Jaime put his hand on Oliver's knee and squeezed it. "You don't need to hire someone to photograph your dick to get a date. If you talk to guys like you have to me, they'll be lining up."

"Guys don't usually want to talk to me for this long, and if they do…" Oliver swallowed hard and looked away. "I already told you what my ex said."

"Man, we do shitty things to each other sometimes." Jaime sighed. "Did he give you any specifics or was it more the parting shot he fired as he slammed the figurative door on your relationship?"

"He wasn't specific, but it wasn't as, uh, dramatic as those metaphors." Oliver let out a deep breath. "We'd been dating for a couple of months and then we finally went to bed together and it wasn't good. I knew it but I was hoping he didn't notice." He shrugged. "Unfortunately, he did notice and he broke up with me right after. That was the end of my one and only relationship."

Nodding, Jaime said, "Killed your confidence, huh?"

"Something like that." The truth was, hearing he was a bad lay from the one guy who had ever shown an interest in him had decimated Oliver's confidence to the point that he had retreated even further into his online world and all but given up on the real one. He hadn't had many friends in Oklahoma City, and he had been living in his parents' basement, working a dead-end job. If he hadn't gotten the offer from Snow Storm to buy his game and hire him, he would still be there, worrying his parents and older sister to death. "I promised myself when I moved here that I'd be different. I've been trying to get out and meet people." Not as hard as he should have been trying, but he had definitely made more of an effort than he had the last several years at home. "If it works and I hit it off with someone…"

"You don't want your lack of confidence to be your downfall," Jaime said, completing his unfinished sentence.

"It's more the lack of skill, but yeah, that's the idea."

"Have you considered sharing this concern with whoever you end up dating and then working through it with him instead of an"—Jaime coughed—"escort?"

Shaking his head, Oliver said, "A person who looks like you can't understand how hard it is to meet someone. Guys probably trip over themselves to get your attention. But me? Finding someone who wants to be with a fat computer geek is harder than hacking into a bank's server. The last thing I need is another strike against me."

"You spend a lot of time hacking banks?" Jaime asked, eyebrows raised.

"No!" Wonderful. Now he'd made himself look like a criminal. "I don't break the law." He paused. "Well, I mean, except for this." He pointed back and forth between them. "And maybe speeding or whatever."

"Got it. Crimes of moral turpitude and traffic violations are fine but cyber-attacks are off the table." Jaime grinned.

Once again, he had managed to sound ridiculous. "Now do you see why nobody's interested in me?" Oliver rubbed his palms over his eyes. "If I weren't paying you, you'd run so fast you wouldn't bother grabbing your clothes before rushing out the door."

"Not true." Jaime shook his head. "Those are my favorite jeans; no chance I'm leaving them behind."

Oliver's eyes widened in surprise and then Jaime grinned.

Relieved that Jaime had been kidding around, Oliver

laughed. "The jeans did look great on you."

"Thanks." Jaime breathed in deeply and then let it out. "Look, you didn't ask my opinion, but I'm going to give it to you anyway." He twisted to the side and grasped Oliver's hand. "We've been talking for going on an hour now so I know you're fun to be with. As far as looks, not everyone wants a guy with a gym body. You're really, really cute, Oliver. If you put yourself out there, you won't have trouble meeting someone who would appreciate what you have to offer and enjoy proving your ex wrong."

Oliver opened his mouth, but Jaime held his hand up and then kept talking.

"But I heard what you said, so I get that you're not at a place where you're comfortable sharing any of the things you told me with someone you want to date."

Relieved, Oliver snapped his mouth shut and nodded.

"Which makes me the lucky man who gets to know the real you and…" Jaime tilted one corner of his mouth up in a wicked grin and then, before Oliver knew what was happening, he surged up, threw one leg over Oliver's, and sat down, resting his ass directly on Oliver's groin. "The even luckier man who gets to fuck you."

Chapter 3

"WHA—" EQUAL PARTS relieved and frazzled, Oliver struggled to get air into his lungs. "What will we do first?"

"Do you have any requests?" Jaime thrust his hips and smiled at Oliver's resulting groan.

"I just…" Another well-placed jab stole Oliver's words and further hardened his dick.

"You just?" Jaime reached over his own shoulder, gripped his T-shirt, and then peeled it off and tossed it behind him.

"Oh my God." Oliver gasped at the sight of Jaime's exposed body. His shoulders were broad and strong, his chest wide and covered in a dusting of dark hair, and ridges were visible on his flat stomach. If Oliver were coding a picture of his ideal man, he could use Jaime as his inspiration model. Better yet, he could toss out the code and snap a photo instead.

"Oliver," Jaime whispered as he leaned forward, once again gifting Oliver with perfect friction where he most wanted it. "Do you have any requests?"

He would have told Jaime to stop moving so they could finish their conversation, but the last thing he wanted was for Jaime to stop moving. "I want to learn what guys like," Oliver said breathlessly.

"Is anything off the table?" Jaime asked, brushing his lips up Oliver's neck, his hot breath ghosting over Oliver's skin.

"Nuh-uh." Partly because Oliver wanted to be good at whatever people enjoyed and partly because he couldn't imagine not enjoying anything with Jaime.

"In that case, let's follow tradition and start at the beginning." Jaime caressed Oliver's forearms, then biceps, and finally his shoulders as he spoke.

"What's the beginning?"

"A kiss."

"I didn't know you'd do something like that," Oliver murmured, more to himself than to Jaime.

"Didn't know meaning you don't want it?" Jaime slid his hands up Oliver's neck. "Or didn't know meaning it's a welcome surprise?" He cupped Oliver's cheeks and gazed into his eyes.

The light and easy touch was as much an invitation as the words. Wanting to know where they'd be going, Oliver whispered, "I want it," and wrapped his arms around Jaime's trim waist.

"Good." Jaime closed the scant distance between them and brushed his lips over Oliver's. "Because I've been wanting to kiss you since I saw you sitting in that bar." He pressed his plush lips to Oliver's for a couple of seconds, pulled back, and then he tilted his head to the side before delving back in. "You're doing great, Oliver."

Initially, Oliver tried to take mental notes about Jaime's technique—how he bracketed Oliver's face with his palms, giving an impression of power and security; how he rubbed his thumbs back and forth over Oliver's cheekbones, showing tenderness and affection; how he intermingled sweet, almost chaste kisses with an occasional flicker of his tongue. But staying focused in the face of Jaime's taste, scent, and touch proved impossible, and soon Oliver forgot all about cataloguing each thing Jaime did and instead succumbed to the pleasure he himself felt.

As if Jaime could sense the change, he shifted gears the moment Oliver relaxed. His kisses, which up to that point had been careful and solicitous, gained an edge as he nibbled and tugged on Oliver's lips. His fingers, which had been gently caressing, slid to the back of Oliver's head, tangled in his hair, and pulled hard enough to give Oliver an additional layer of sensation without causing pain. And his thrusting upgraded to a hard grind as he rutted against Oliver's dick, giving him the best kind of friction. None of Oliver's admittedly limited previous sexual encounters held a candle to that moment, sitting in bed, underwear on, kissing and humping like a teenager.

It felt so good, in fact, that he was seconds from coming, so, as much as he hated to do it, he yanked himself away from the best kiss of his life and buried his face against Jaime's neck. "I'm close," he groaned, trailing his fingertips up Jaime's flank and across his back. "And I don't want this to end yet."

"It doesn't have to end." Jaime massaged Oliver's neck. "Let yourself enjoy it. At your age, you'll be able to go again in twenty minutes."

The mention of time reminded Oliver why he was there and, more importantly, why Jaime was there. He twisted his head to the side, looking for a clock. When he didn't see it on one nightstand, he turned to look at the other one.

"What're you doing?"

"Trying to see how much time we have left."

His forehead crinkling, Jaime said, "I'm not in a rush."

"The ATM had a three-hundred dollar limit so I can only pay for three hours." It was nine fifteen. They had both gotten to the bar early so he had probably used an hour and a half of his time already.

"I see." Jaime climbed off Oliver's lap, took in a deep breath, and rubbed his lips together. "I forgot to tell you that after two hours, my rate gets cut in half."

"Really?" Oliver thought back to his conversation with the escort agency. "The guy on the phone didn't mention that."

"Right." Jaime cleared his throat. "Well, the thing is, I'm going to take this off the books."

"What does that mean?" Oliver scrunched his eyebrows.

"You said earlier that you know about the two-hour minimum?" For the first time, Jaime sounded uncertain, maybe even nervous.

Oliver nodded.

"I'll tell the agency that's how long we spent, give them their cut, and handle the rest of the time solo."

"So even though I'm paying less, you'll still make the same amount?"

"That's right." Jaime smiled, looking pleased. He turned sideways and laid his hand on Oliver's chest. "See? We have plenty of time."

Either whatever had been bothering Jaime moments earlier was no longer an issue or Oliver had misread him.

"You won't get in trouble?" he asked, still concerned about the odd shift in Jaime's demeanor.

"Not if you don't tell them," Jaime said, his tone once again playful.

"I won't say anything. I promise." Even if Jaime no longer seemed worried about whatever it was he had been thinking about a minute earlier, Oliver had seen enough crime shows where prostitutes were beaten or murdered by their pimps to consider the risks in Jaime's line of work very serious.

"Now that that's settled"—Jaime curled his palm around the side of Oliver's face and leaned toward him—"let's go back to what we were doing."

With Jaime no longer on his lap and the concerns from their conversation fresh in his mind, Oliver had trouble slipping back into the zone of mindless pleasure. Thankfully, in addition to being skilled, Jaime was patient. He didn't speak or hurry them along, choosing instead to go back to gentle kisses and nearly platonic touches. Soon they both lay on their sides, hands exploring, tongues tangling, and hips undulating. Following Jaime's lead was easy, natural, and somewhere along the way, Oliver stopped worrying and thinking, all his energy focused on feeling.

Slipping his hand under Oliver's shirt, Jaime whispered, "Mmm, you're warm." He caressed Oliver's flank and back. "And you have great skin. Soft and smooth."

"I like how you feel too." Oliver put one palm on Jaime's defined pectoral and skated the other over his bulging bicep. "Muscular," he rasped.

"I work out a lot." Jaime smoothed his hand up to Oliver's shoulder and then slowly moved it over his side and onto his stomach.

"It shows." As did the fact that Oliver spent no time at the gym, but he managed to stop himself from saying that out loud. No reason to state the obvious.

"Let's get this shirt off." Jaime gently pushed Oliver's shirt up his torso.

Part of Oliver wanted to protest. After all, his fat belly would play no part in sex, so why did he need to expose it? But he had read on Reddit that constant insecurity was not an attractive quality, so he nodded, sat up, and let Jaime undress him.

To Oliver's relief, Jaime showed no indication of being bothered by his body. He supposed Jaime dealt with people of all shapes and sizes in his line of work. That thought led to another.

"Are you… You're gay, right?" Oliver scrunched his forehead. "Or at least bi?"

Arching his eyebrows, Jaime blinked. "I'm in bed with you right now and we're both men." He said each word slowly.

"Right, but I mean, this could be one of those gay for pay things, right?"

For several seconds, Jaime stared at him, his mouth open but no words coming out. Then he threw his head back and laughed. "You're something else." He shook his head and rose to a kneeling position. "We haven't been apart since we met so you know I haven't popped any pills." He tucked his thumbs into the waistband of his underwear, shoved it down, and then cupped his erection. "This hard dick is courtesy of you. No chemical enhancement." He lay back down and kicked the underwear off. "So yes, I'm gay, and yes, you turn me on."

Completely distracted from his earlier question, Oliver darted his eyes from Jaime's groin to his face and back again. "You're gorgeous with your clothes on but like this…" Staring at Jaime's long, thick shaft and large balls stole Oliver's breath. "Wow."

"You said you want to know what guys like," Jaime said, his voice husky. "The way you're looking at me right now…" He shivered. "I like it."

"How—" Oliver swallowed down the thickness in his throat. "How am I looking at you?"

"Like you want me. A lot."

"I do." Oliver stared at Jaime's dick again, noticing that it looked even bigger. "You're perfect." Jaimie's shaft was straight, the veins subtle, and his glans rose-colored. Oliver's mouth watered and his fingers twitched looking at it.

"You can touch me." Jaime grasped his erection and pointed it up, offering himself to Oliver.

"You'll tell me if I do it wrong?" Oliver reached for Jaime's shaft as he spoke, his fingertips making contact with the smooth, soft skin.

"Yes, but—" Jaime curled his fingers around Oliver's wrist and waited for him to look him in the eyes before continuing to speak. "I get that your ex screwed with your head and that you don't have a lot of experience with other guys, but you've got at least fifteen years of masturbating under your belt, right?"

Though he wriggled uncomfortably at the blunt language, Oliver nodded.

"It's just a cock." Jaime covered Oliver's hand with his own and moved it over his shaft. "You know how to make yourself feel good. I'm not any different."

The explanation made sense and Oliver relaxed. "Okay."

Smiling gently, Jaime tapped his fingers up Oliver's arm, over to his side, and onto his hip. He stretched his hand out, grazing Oliver's balls through his boxers. "When you're ready for me to touch you, let me know."

Breath catching and skin tingling, Oliver dipped his head in agreement. Part of him wanted nothing more than Jaime's touch anywhere and everywhere, especially on his dick. But, if Jaime touched him there, he would forget everything else he wanted to do, and he didn't want anything to interfere with what had turned into the most erotic moment of his life.

"I didn't expect it to be like this," he whispered to himself as he loosely stroked Jaime's shaft.

"Like what?"

"I don't know." He slid his thumb over Jaime's crown, and

when Jaime's breath hitched in response, Oliver's entire body shuddered. "So hot, I guess."

"Are we talking about the hand job?" Jaime asked. His voice was tight but he made no move to interfere with Oliver's ministrations or move him along.

"Yeah and everything else." Oliver slipped his hand lower and curled it over Jaime's balls. They were larger than his own and warmer. He wanted to crawl down the mattress and bury his face in them. "I set this night up so I could learn and now I'm..." He shook his head, not sure how to articulate his thoughts and not interested enough to focus on them.

"That's a perfect reaction."

"Uh-huh," Oliver said agreeably despite not knowing what Jaime meant. At that moment it didn't matter. "I wish I could touch every part of you all at once."

"I'll help." Jaime tipped onto his back, grabbed Oliver's free hand, and moved it to his groin.

The angle was a little awkward, but with Jaime lying on his back and Oliver tucked into his side, he was able to caress Jaime's balls with one hand and stroke his shaft with the other. And although his own dick was getting no stimulation, with each slide of his hand over Jaime's erection, his own arousal climbed.

"Still want me to keep my hands to myself?" Jaime asked, his voice hoarse.

"Uh-huh." Oliver quickened his pace, his groin tightening. "If you touched me like this, I'd have lost it already." He looked at Jaime's chest and dipped his head toward it. "You have a lot of staying power."

"Benefit of age," Jaime bit out. "Plus, I don't want to end your fun."

Glancing up, Oliver noticed Jaime's expression matched his strained voice. His nostrils were flared, his jaw clenched, and the veins on the sides of his neck throbbed. The visual proof that Jaime was affected by what he was doing ramped up Oliver's confidence and encouraged him to go further.

"Jaime?"

"Yes?"

"Can I…" Oliver leaned closer, his eyes locked on Jaime's heaving chest—broad, muscular, sprinkled with brown hair, and topped by small, tan nipples. His limited sexual experience hadn't given Oliver an opportunity to explore another man's chest and it wasn't an area of the body he focused on in his fantasies, but now that he had an up-close view of Jaime's nipples, he was struck with the urge to lick and suck.

"Can you what?"

Oliver glanced at Jaime's face, down to his nipples, and back up again.

Following Oliver's gaze, understanding dawned on Jaime's face. "God, yes." He wrapped his big hand around the back of Oliver's head and tugged him forward. "They're really sensitive so anything you do will feel amazing to me."

The first thing Oliver did was press his face against Jaime's skin and inhale. Overlaid with soap or body wash was the scent of Jaime's musk. Clean but rich, it made Oliver's balls tighten and throb. He was taking whiff after whiff, moaning, and thrusting his erection against Jaime's leg when he realized what he was doing. His neck heating, Oliver jerked his eyes up to Jaime's face. To his relief, there no censure in Jaime's expression so he continued exploring, nuzzling his way up Jaime's sternum to the base of his throat and then licking a path down to his nipple.

The texture changed when he reached the areola, the skin softer and smoother. After a few licks, it drew up, crinkling into a firm pebble. Oliver flicked the tip of his tongue against the nub, enjoying the sensation. Wanting to know if it'd feel different, he flattened his tongue and swiped the top of it against the nipple.

"Ungh," Jaime moaned, tightening his grip on Oliver's hair.

Proud of his accomplishment, Oliver moved to the other nipple, and this time, instead of just using his tongue, he covered it with his entire mouth and sucked.

"Yes, like that." Jaime bucked his hips and tugged Oliver's hair, pulling him closer.

Still holding Jaime's thick shaft in one hand and cradling his warm balls in the other, Oliver suckled on his nipple. He lost himself in the scent and taste of the man beside him, sucking, nibbling, and licking his way from one nub to the other and then, wanting to draw in more of Jaime's enticing flavor, he shifted further to the side and breathed him in as he lapped at his armpit.

"Oh, damn," Jaime panted as he raised his left arm, making more of himself available to Oliver.

Raising his gaze, Oliver said, "Not too weird?"

"No." Jaime shook his head and combed his fingers through Oliver's hair. "I'm not sure anyone has ever smelled me quite that intensely or licked me there but it's sexy as hell."

"Yeah?" Oliver's chest lightened.

Nodding, Jaime said, "Very sexy."

"Thanks, I…" Oliver lowered his voice. "I'm really enjoying this."

"I am too." Jaime's tone was sincere and his smile reached his eyes, the skin next to them crinkling.

"Good," Oliver said, relieved. Paying someone to teach him the fundamentals of sex had seemed like a great idea when Oliver had made the appointment, but now that he had spent time with Jaime, he realized something that should have been obvious—the person he was hiring was a person—and forcing himself on someone repulsed him, even if the force was through his wallet. "If I do something you don't like, tell me."

"I already promised I'd do that." Jaime continued tenderly combing his fingers through Oliver's hair.

"I know, but that was about me learning. This is…" He tried to think of the right words. "I'll pay you no matter what we do or don't do, okay? You don't have to put up with something you don't like because you're worried about money."

Lines forming on his forehead, Jaime opened his mouth but then instead of speaking, he ran his tongue over his lips, swallowed, and took a deep breath. "I'm not worried about money, and you have my word that if you do anything I don't like, I'll tell you."

Trusting Jaime to keep his promise, Oliver returned his focus to the gorgeous body in front of him. Never before had an experience triggered all of his senses at once, and he relished every aspect: the sight of Jaime's face rapt with pleasure, the sound of his aroused moans, his musky scent, the feeling of his hard dick, and the taste of his skin and sweat. Oliver was so lost in enjoying Jaime, that he lost track of his own body until the sensation of a rapidly approaching orgasm hit him.

"Oh." He sucked in a surprised breath and stilled his hips, which had been instinctively humping Jaime's leg. "I—" He drew in more air and willed his body to calm down. "I'm going to—"

Before he knew what was happening, Jaime surged up, rolled

him onto his back, and slammed his mouth on Oliver's. As he jammed his tongue past Oliver's lips, he shoved his hand under Oliver's boxers and gripped his shaft.

The pleasure was sharp, sudden, and all consuming. Within seconds, Oliver was screaming into Jaime's mouth and shooting into his palm as his vision went black. "Oh God." Oliver gasped for air, his chest heaving and his entire body trembling. "That was—" He swallowed, getting moisture into his dry throat. "That was—" He opened his eyes and stared at Jaime in awe.

"For me too."

"Did you…"

"I did." Jaime held up his cum-coated palm before wiping it on the sheet. "And it was a great one."

Needing to be certain he understood, Oliver tipped his chin toward Jaime's hand and asked, "That was from both of us?"

Jaime nodded. "The second you were done, I finished myself off." He lay on his side, draped his arm around Oliver, and rubbed his hip. "I barely needed a stroke to get there because you already had me on the edge."

"I did?"

"You're incredibly sensual." Jaime's gentle fingers roamed up Oliver's side and onto his stomach. "The way you were touching me—" He let out a deep breath and shook his head. "It was all I could do to hold myself together."

"I'm not even sure what I did," Oliver admitted. "I forgot to concentrate."

"Maybe that's the trick."

"Not concentrating?" Oliver asked, confused.

"Feeling and doing instead of thinking and worrying."

"I can't help that. When I want to do something well, I focus on it and work hard until I get it right."

"You got it exactly right, Oliver. *Exactly* right. Follow your instincts and you'll have nothing to worry about."

Oliver chewed on his lip and sighed.

"That was a compliment." Jaime curled his free hand around Oliver's neck and looked at him worriedly. "Why don't you seem happy?"

Letting out a frustrated breath, Oliver said, "Because it's different with you. I know if I do anything wrong, you'll tell me and you won't get upset and it won't ruin anything, so I can forget and feel and do and whatever. But that won't work in real life."

"I see."

Silently, Jaime continued caressing him and Oliver realized he was touching his stomach. His big, soft, flabby stomach. During his few sexual encounters, Oliver had made sure to strategically place the blanket to limit exposure of his unappealing body, so now having such an unattractive part of himself seen and touched was disconcerting.

"Feels nothing like your body, huh?" he asked, trying to hide his discomfort behind humor. "No hard muscles."

"We have different builds." Jaime curled his fingers in and out, feeling every inch of Oliver's waist and stomach. "I happen to prefer the fullness of yours."

Taking him at his word, Oliver relaxed and let himself enjoy Jaime's touch. Even though he hadn't accomplished the goal he had set going into the night, he had no regrets. Nor was he ready to give up. He wasn't rolling in money, but he had enough to afford more time with Jaime.

"Would it be okay with you if we do this again?" Oliver asked tentatively.

His face brightening, Jaime said, "That's a good idea."

"Thanks. I'll call the agency and make an appointment for next weekend."

"No, don't do that," Jaime snapped.

"Oh." Disappointment slammed into Oliver. "I'm so—"

"I'll give you my number so you can get in touch with me directly." Jaime averted his gaze and cleared his throat. "That way you can save a little money."

Jaime's body was tense, his expression not nearly as happy as it had been seconds earlier.

"You're sure?" Oliver asked. "Because you seem—"

"Yes." Jaime sighed. "I'm very sure." He dipped his face and brushed his lips over Oliver's. "Maybe if you keep seeing how great you are at it, you'll be more confident."

Or he could force himself to focus next time and actually learn something. Either way, he would get to spend another evening with Jaime. Happiness unfurled in Oliver's chest at the prospect. Life was looking up.

Chapter 4

S NOW STORM, LTD. favored an open-concept workspace with
no walls or dividers between the simple white worktables. It
was supposed to breed a friendly and collegial environment,
which Oliver supposed was true, but it made focusing a
challenge. In the two months he had been there, he had learned
that most people wore headphones and listened to music to
block out the noise around them. He did that occasionally, but
music distracted him when he was working on detail work, so if
he really needed to focus, he took advantage of his ability to get
lost in his own head and tune out everyone and everything but
his screen.

"Looks like someone had a great weekend."

Not realizing the comment was directed at him, Oliver
stared at his screen, trying to see where he had gone wrong in his
design of yet another fight sequence. Action wasn't his favorite
genre, he preferred strategy, but his boss had assigned him this
project, so he was going to build the best fighting game in Snow
Storm history.

A throat cleared behind him and a hand landed on his
shoulder. "Earth to Oliver. Come in, Oliver."

Blinking in surprise, he twisted his head to look behind him.
"Oh. Hi, Tamra."

"Hey. My eyes are blurry and my brain is fuzzy, so I'm taking a coffee and muffin break. Want to come with me?"

Oliver had never been the type to make friends easily or quickly, and it seemed as if many people who worked on his floor had the same problem, but Tamra Johnson was an exception. Her pierced lip was constantly turned up in a smile, her purple-tinted-contact-lensed eyes were always bright, and her booming laugh often bounced off the exposed brick walls. It was impossible not to like Tamra. During his first week, he had found himself in the elevator with her, both of them heading downstairs for coffee. He had been intimidated at first. Tamra exuded confidence, her posture, her tone, even her hair. He didn't know anyone else who could pull off the faux hawk she wore in her curly black hair. But she had smiled and chatted with him the entire way to Starbucks and back. After that, she made a point of inviting him along when she went on coffee runs, and he now considered her a friend.

"Yeah, I could use a reload." He saved his work. "Stepping away from this for a few minutes will probably help me get some perspective on it." He got up and rubbed his palms over his eyes. "What are the chances they're not out of chocolate croissants?"

"Well, it's"—she looked at her phone as they walked toward the elevator—"four twenty-seven so I'd say about thirty-five percent."

"Yeah," Oliver sighed resignedly. "You're probably right."

Laughing, she said, "I'm sure they'll have something in stock that you can tolerate."

He patted his round stomach. "I'm sure you're right."

They stepped into the elevator, and Tamra pressed the button for the lobby. "You didn't answer my question about your weekend."

"What question?"

"You've been humming and smiling all day." She nudged her

shoulder against his arm. "I take it this means you met someone special in our fair city?"

Feeling heat crawl up his neck, Oliver dropped his gaze and squirmed.

"You're blushing! That means I'm right." She laughed delightedly. "Go you! Tell me all about the lucky lady." The elevator dinged and Tamra stepped outside with Oliver following her.

One nice thing about his life in Oklahoma was that the few people he knew already knew him. Moving to a new place meant meeting new people, which meant coming out all over again. He had planned to brush off Tamra's comment, partly because talking about his personal life made him uncomfortable and partly because he hadn't so much *met* someone as he had *hired* someone, but he didn't want to find himself back in the closet so he sucked in a deep breath and said, "Not a lady. A gentleman."

"Oh." Tamra's steps faltered for a second and then she regained her footing and grabbed his forearm as they walked into the Starbucks. "I'm sorry for assuming. Asshole move on my part. Tell me about the lucky gentleman."

Although her reaction relieved Oliver, his shoulders remained tense at the prospect of his work colleague finding out he had hired an escort. "Not much to tell."

"That is a horrible bragging technique." They stepped up to the counter. "You're supposed to tell me about how hard you hit that ass or whatever." She turned to the blue-haired barista, ignored his shocked expression, and said, "I'll have a cinnamon dolce latte, grande, and a chocolate chunk muffin."

By the time it was Oliver's turn to order, he was hopeful his skin had returned to its regular non-red color. "Venti iced coffee with milk and two pumps of sweetener, please. And a chocolate croissant."

"Sorry, we're out of croissants."

After settling for a cheese Danish and paying for his food, Oliver joined Tamra at the end of the counter where she waited for her drink and picked at her muffin.

"So, continuing our conversation—"

Oliver groaned and retrieved his Danish from the small brown bag.

"I can see that you're uncomfortable, so I'll stop poking into your dating life."

"Thanks." He took a bite.

"But—"

He groaned again.

"Cut it out." She whacked him lightly on the arm. "But," she said again, this time with more emphasis, "I get that our industry isn't the most welcoming of anyone who isn't a straight, white wannabe-bro dude, but if it's fallout at work you're worried about, you should know that won't be a problem for you at Snow Storm."

"Good diversity policies?" He had been given endless links to policies and forms when he signed on with the company, but he hadn't read most of it.

"I don't know. Probably." Tamra shrugged as she reached for one of the cups the barista had just set down. "But that's not what I mean." She handed Oliver his drink and then picked up her own cup, leaned close to him, and whispered conspiratorial-ly, "Have you heard about the owners?"

"What owners?"

"Oh, you haven't!" She smiled broadly and bounced on the fronts of her feet. "I love being the bearer of new gossip!"

She was silly and nosy and maybe even a little brash, but she was also friendly, didn't look down on him, and made him feel included, so Oliver laughed along with her. "Go ahead. Get it off your chest. What's the gossip?"

"Let's sit for a minute. I don't want to talk about this in the office."

Taking the last bite of his Danish, Oliver nodded and followed her to a small table.

"Okay," she said breathily and leaned forward. "The company is run by Jack Storm."

"Uh huh." Oliver nodded at the information he already knew.

"But Jack is only one of the owners." She said the sentence like it was a revelation.

"Right. The other is James Snow."

Tamra frowned. "You said you didn't know the gossip."

"The names of Snow Storm's owners aren't gossip."

"Fine, but Jack Storm is the one who speaks at the big company meetings and signs all the public stuff so most people haven't heard of Snow. Who knew you'd done so much due diligence on your new employer?" She tore off a piece of muffin, popped it in her mouth, and then tipped her cup against her lips.

He hadn't actually done much of anything except jump up and down and accept the first offer they'd made him. But James Snow was the author of Oliver's coding textbook so he knew he had founded the gaming company.

"I don't want to hurt your feelings or anything, but your gossip could use a little more gossip."

Tamra snorted and then coughed. "Quit being funny when I'm drinking." She wiped the back of her hand across her mouth and coughed again. "You almost made me drown in my latte."

"That would have been quite a feat."

"Do you want to hear the gossip or not?"

Oliver arched his eyebrows and sipped his coffee.

"Don't answer that question. I'm telling you anyway." She coughed again, took another drink, and said, "So the rumor is that Snow and Storm were together together, as in a couple. They founded the company and then, when they broke up, Snow went silent partner or whatever and Storm stayed on."

"They're gay?" Not that it mattered. The personal life of his boss's boss's boss, or however high up that chain needed to go to reach the owners, had no impact on Oliver. But he was still happy to hear that someone like him, even in a small way, owned and operated one of the most successful independently owned gaming companies in the industry.

"That's the rumor." Tamra shrugged. "So you probably don't need to worry about people finding out you're gay."

"I'm not in the closet."

"No?" She ate another piece of her muffin. "Then spill the beans about the hotty you met this weekend."

How being out translated to broadcasting details about his personal life, Oliver didn't know, but he didn't think Tamra meant any harm with her question so instead of pointing that out, he said, "There's nothing to tell."

"Fine be that way." She crumpled up her muffin bag and napkin and stuffed them dramatically into her now empty cup. "Just kidding." She smiled and stood. "I was hoping to live vicariously through someone who can actually get a good date. I'll just have to go home and watch a loop of rom-coms on Netflix to get my fix."

"Doesn't your husband take you out?" Oliver got up and walked with her to the door.

"Oh crap." Tamra stopped walking and grimaced. "The gay

thing took down all my defenses." She twisted the gold band around her ring finger. "I really have to be careful about that."

"About what?"

She sighed. "The husband thing isn't true."

"What?" Oliver furrowed his brow.

"So…you can't tell anyone, okay? But I'm not married. Never have been. I made that up."

"Why?"

She sucked in a deep breath and then let it out. "Because when I started my first job in Seattle, I was twenty-two, decent-looking, and female. Apparently that gave every asshole I worked with permission to hit on me and then treat me like crap when I turned him down."

"They did that?"

"All the time," she said. "Being one of the only black people in the room is hard enough. I can't tell you how often I was left out of decisions and workgroups because some overly sensitive man decided my saying no to sleeping with him meant I wasn't a team player. It sucked so much I had to use up all my lives just to get through a workday until, eventually, I was like, fuck this shit, and I told the next guy who hit on me that I had a boyfriend. That actually worked surprisingly well, so I kept up with it. The industry isn't that big and everyone knows everyone, so I stuck to the story at my next job and the one after that. At some point it seemed like the pretend boyfriend and I had been together long enough that we should get engaged and then when my family took a trip to Hawaii over Christmas one year, I told everyone we got married in a small ceremony."

"How long ago was that?" Oliver asked, shocked.

"Let's see." She looked up and twisted her lips. "It'll be four years this Christmas."

"And in four plus years they haven't figured out that nobody has met your husband?"

"My backstory is that he's in sales and he has to travel all the time for work, so he can't make it to anything where SOs are invited. I have a picture on my phone of me and my cousin at a luau from that Hawaii trip, and I pull it up if anyone wants to see my husband." She shook her head. "The truth is, they don't actually care about my husband. They just feel like a no from a woman means nothing, but keeping off another guy's turf is sacrosanct."

"That's terrible."

"I know." She sighed. "It still happens, but I think the wedding band keeps most of the dirtbags away."

"I don't know what to say." He truly didn't.

"Just don't tell people my husband is imaginary and we're good."

"I won't," he promised. He hadn't seen anyone being inappropriate with Tamra at work, but maybe that was because of her pretend husband or maybe it was because he rarely paid attention to anything but his screen. "So what's your long-term plan with this thing? Are you planning on getting an imaginary divorce at some point?"

"I have no idea." She shrugged and shook her head. "I shouldn't have to lie about having a man in my life to get people to take me seriously at work, but the results speak for themselves, and it's not like I want to hang out with those guys outside of the office anyway, so whatever."

"And here I thought you were the friendliest person in the office and you liked everyone."

"I try to be friendly and I do like most of the people we work with, but we have like twenty-five designers on our floor and only three of us are women." She cleared her throat and breathed in. "The last game I worked on had a special ops team killing zombies and the single female soldier looked like a porn star. Big hair, tons of makeup, boobs up to her chin. It feels like I'm in a men's locker room or a frat house or something. I'm not saying all guys are assholes or anything, but it's not a super-comfortable environment." She bit her lip. "It's hard to explain."

"I get what you're saying." He made a mental note to talk to his project team about reworking the clothing on their female warrior, who currently looked exactly the way Tamra had described. "And I understand what it feels like to be on the outside."

"You're a good guy, Oliver." She squared her shoulders. "We better get back in there. The games aren't going to design themselves."

Chapter 5

"HOW WAS YOUR week?" Oliver closed the hotel room door behind Jaime and then followed him back into the room.

"Good," Jaime said as he slipped off his jacket and laid it beside Oliver's on the seat of the desk chair. "How was yours?"

"Fine." Oliver shifted from one socked foot to the other and watched Jaime toe off his brown leather loafers. "Sorry this hotel isn't as nice as the last couple of Fridays."

When he had chosen the Bookstore as his first meeting place with an escort, booking a room at the hotel above the bar had made sense. The second time they had met, Oliver had stuck to that system, not wanting to mess with a good thing. When he scheduled this appointment—the third in as many weeks—Oliver admitted to himself that he wanted Jaime to become a regular part of his weekends, and even though he was earning more than he had his entire life, he was also living on his own in a very expensive city, trying to build a savings account, and paying for Jaime's time. Spending two hundred and fifty dollars for a hotel room strained his finances uncomfortably, so he had found an alternative.

"The hotel is fine." Jaime smiled, raised his hand, and curled his fingers inward in a beckoning motion. "Come here."

Rubbing his lips together, Oliver shuffled closer to him. "There was a Groupon for this one so it was less than half the price of the Alexis."

Rather than acknowledging Oliver's excuse, Jaime focused on his rambling. "You're nervous."

Not sure how to respond, Oliver didn't.

"It's just the two of us here, same as the last two times. We both know what to expect from each other, and we both feel confident about being able to meet those expectations, right?"

Oliver considered Jaime's words and then sighed in relief. "Right." Tension left his body and his shoulders relaxed. "Sorry. I was acting like this is a date or something." He shook his head and smiled at his own foolishness. "It's silly for me to be nervous with you."

"Exactly." Jaime curled his arm around Oliver's waist. "We have this arrangement so you won't worry."

"I know." Oliver flattened his palm on Jaime's chest and leaned against him. Most men wouldn't be able to support Oliver's meaty frame, but Jaime was strong enough to hold him up. "I guess I forgot for a second."

His voice lowering and deepening, Jaime said, "I've got the perfect way to remind you."

The memories of the evening he had spent with Jaime had occupied Oliver's mind all week. Like they had the first night together, they had talked, laughed, and touched. Oliver had even had the pleasure of stroking Jaime off, saying he wanted to try out the lesson Jaime had taught him. But as much as he had enjoyed those memories, they didn't hold a candle to the reality of the soft lips that now brushed against his, the firm fingers that dug into his back, and the hot breath that ghosted across his face. Once again losing himself in the moment, Oliver clutched Jaime's shirt and closed his eyes.

"You feel good," Jaime whispered as he grazed his hands up

Oliver's back.

Bodies pressed together and hands wandering above the waistline, they stood in the hotel room and exchanged chaste kisses. Jaime didn't seem to be in any hurry, but after a couple of minutes, Oliver's arousal climbed and his hips instinctively began rocking.

"Jaime," he moaned and grasped Jaime's shoulders tightly. Forgetting to be nervous about making a wrong move, he flicked his tongue at the seam of Jaime's lips and slid it into his mouth. Like Jaime's scent, his taste burrowed through Oliver's entire body and heated him up. "You taste good." It wasn't a flavor Oliver could identify—not toothpaste or gum or coffee—but Oliver thought he might be addicted to it already.

"So do you." Jaime twirled his tongue around Oliver's and then sucked on it as he threaded his fingers through Oliver's hair.

"Mmm," Oliver moaned, rubbing his hands up and down Jaime's muscular arms. "I don't know how you do this to me so easily."

"What am I doing to you?" Jaime hunched down, nosed Oliver's head to the side, and nibbled his way down his neck.

"I usually obsess over a million random things, but you somehow take me completely out of my own head."

"You're a smart guy, which is really sexy, so I don't want to stop all that thinking but maybe a break now and then is a good idea." As if to ensure that break would continue at that very moment, Jaime pushed Oliver's sweater collar aside, flattened his tongue at the juncture of Oliver's neck and shoulder, and then swiped it up to his ear. "Is there anything in particular you want to do tonight?" Jaime nipped Oliver's earlobe. "Anything you've been hoping to try?"

During his alone time in bed and in the shower, Oliver had thought about a variety of things he would love to try with Jaime. But no single fantasy took center stage over the others, and the only consistency between them was Jaime's presence.

"Is it bad if I say no?" Oliver drew in a deep breath. "Not 'no' as in I don't want to try anything, but 'no' as in I'm good with whatever."

Pulling his head back, Jaime looked into Oliver's eyes. "Why would that be bad?"

"I don't know." Oliver shrugged and flicked his gaze away from Jaime's. "People like decisiveness and firmness or whatever." He looked up at Jaime from underneath his lashes. "Right?"

"Well." Jaime grinned devilishly, and before Oliver realized he'd moved his hand, long fingers wrapped around his dick through his jeans and squeezed. "You're plenty firm."

"Ah." Oliver shouted in surprise and jumped away. He blinked rapidly as his brain caught up with what was happening and then he pushed himself back against Jaime's palm. "Uh." He coughed. "That's not what I meant by firm."

"I know what you meant." Jaime cupped Oliver's groin again and slid his hand up and down. "And I think once your confidence is built up, you'll be more comfortable taking the lead. In the meantime, I have some great ideas to get us by."

"What ideas?" Oliver shifted closer to Jaime, circled his arms around his waist, and rested his head on his chest. "I like ideas."

"I'm an idea man myself." Jaime gave Oliver's erection another squeeze and then slid his hands around to his butt. "Based on our last couple of times together, I've gotten the sense that you're big on tastes and scents."

In his head flashed the image of Jaime's chest and armpits, which he had licked and smelled both times they had been together. Heat climbed up the back of his neck, and he was thankful Jaime continued speaking rather than waiting for him to respond.

"A great way to get both of those things is a blow job."

The term blow job had Oliver's breath catching and his testicles rising closer to his groin. "I can do that." He gulped. "Should I, uh, just get on my knees here or do you want to be in bed for it?"

Jaime laughed under his breath, but the warmth of his touch and the kindness in his eyes kept Oliver from being offended. "My thought is we both take off our clothes and get in bed." He kneaded Oliver's backside. "Some guys aren't into sixty-nines because getting done distracts them from doing or they want all their focus on their own dick when it's getting sucked, but—" He leaned down and nipped at Oliver's chin. The move was more playful than erotic, and it helped slow Oliver's racing heart. "I'm thinking it'll be fun to go at it together. If I do something you like, you can try it on me. Or if there's something you want to try, you can go for it, and I can do it to you so you see how it feels." Jaime arched his eyebrows and grinned playfully. "Who said fun and learning can't mix?"

Fun was a great word to describe Jaime. He was also kind, sharp, and scorchingly sexy. Oliver wanted to ask why such a handsome, personable, and intelligent man was selling his body for what was effectively fifty dollars an hour. Wanted to, but didn't. Maybe Jaime needed the money. Maybe sex for pay was his kink. Maybe he was bored. Whatever the reason, there was no way to ask a question like that without coming across as judgmental, and besides, paying Jaime to sleep with him didn't entitle him to Jaimie's personal business, so Oliver kept his questions to himself.

"I'm on board with that plan." With what they were doing established, Oliver began stripping off his clothes. Getting naked in front of Jaime was easier the third time around. He had already seen Oliver's heavy body and that hadn't kept him from coming back again or seemingly enjoying himself. A couple of minutes later, Oliver climbed into the bed nude and Jaime followed him.

"What's first?" Oliver asked.

"If I wrote out a step-by-step list, you'd follow it, wouldn't you?"

"Sure." Oliver bobbed his head. "I'd love directions to follow. But I don't think it works that way, does it?"

"Nope." Settling on his side, Jaime shoved a folded pillow under his head and rested his hand on Oliver's hip. "You're a gamer, right?"

"Uh-huh."

"When you're playing a game, what's your favorite moment?"

The obvious answer would be winning, but that wasn't actually the best part of playing a game. "Figuring out how to get around the challenging parts, especially if it's in a way that isn't obvious."

Dipping his chin in agreement, Jaime said, "Going to bed with someone is a lot like that. Not the challenging thing, but the navigating. It's fun to touch and explore and figure out what he's into. Even after you're with the same guy for a long time, you can find new ways to play by dropping in things you know he'll love when you know he doesn't expect them."

"Like an Easter egg," Oliver said, continuing the gaming analogy.

"Exactly." Jaime smiled broadly and rubbed Oliver's flank.

"That makes sense." Oliver scooted closer to Jaime, wanting to feel his heat, his skin.

"Good." Jaime cupped Oliver's cheek, dropped his head forward, and brushed his lower lip across Oliver's mouth.

That unexpected and erotic take on a kiss made Oliver gasp. As soon as his lips parted, Jaime returned, this time dragging his lip first over Oliver's lower lip and then his upper lip. He repeated the action from one side of Oliver's mouth to the other, his pace unhurried. Oliver swallowed hard but otherwise didn't move, not wanting to disrupt Jaime's unusual seduction.

"You have a beautiful face, you know that?" Jaime rasped as he moved his thumb across Oliver's eyebrow. "So handsome." He ran his gaze over Oliver's face and traced his cheekbone with his thumb. "I could look at you all day."

Oliver was nothing special, average on a good day, but the awe in Jaime's voice and the appreciation in his eyes made him think maybe, just maybe, he had been selling himself a little short.

"Your skin," Jaime said appreciatively. He dragged his lips from the top of Oliver's cheekbone down to his chin and then licked a swath back up. "So smooth and soft."

"I... I shaved before I came here."

"Not all over, thankfully." Jaime gently brushed the back of his hand over Oliver's groin. "I'm glad you don't wax or shave your hair off."

"I've thought about it," Oliver confessed. "But I was worried I'd cut myself or get razor burn or it'd be itchy when it grew back. Plus, I wasn't sure if that was only a porn thing or a real life thing." He looked down at Jaime's hand gently petting an area nobody usually saw, let alone touched, and waited for the awkward feelings to come. Oddly enough, they didn't. "So, uh, that's why I just leave it alone."

"It's not only a porn thing. Some guys keep themselves bare or trimmed to almost nothing, but like I said—" Jaime pushed his fingertips through Oliver's pubic bush. "I'm into the hair." He kept going until he reached Oliver's balls and then he caressed them. "The natural look does it for me way more than obsessive sculpting."

"You're really good at making people feel comfortable in uncomfortable situations," Oliver observed.

Smiling, Jaime wedged his nose under Oliver's chin, pushed it up, and then kissed his throat. "Is this an uncomfortable situation?"

"No." Oliver arched his neck, giving Jaime more room. "It should be, but you make it okay. It's a talent."

"You're sweet." Jaime flicked his tongue against Oliver's earlobe and then sucked on it while he continued handling Oliver's balls. Moving his hand up Oliver's shaft, he said, "You're also hard enough to pop." He bit Oliver's shoulder and rubbed his thumb over Oliver's glans. "Let's get this show on the road."

Dropping kisses, licks, and nibbles along the way, Jaime shifted around until his erection bobbed in front of Oliver's face. Unable to stop himself, Oliver leaned forward and inhaled deeply. The musky scent of man and arousal permeated the air, fogging his brain and sending his heart into overdrive. He got closer, nuzzling Jaime's balls and moaning.

Brushing his fingers over Oliver's head, Jaime breathlessly said, "You make me forget myself."

Oliver would have answered but he could barely understand what Jaime was saying and forming words was nowhere near possible; his entire focus rested on the thick shaft that was close enough to smell, touch, and lick. Before he could get his mouth on his prize, wet heat surrounded his own dick.

"Oh God." There had been no warm up, no introductory licks or light fondling. Instead, Jaime had sucked his shaft completely into his mouth. "I…" His balls drew up so quickly, he wasn't sure he could keep himself from climaxing. "Jaime." The hand that had been gently playing with his testicles closed around them and tugged, saving him from falling over the edge. "Oh God." He dropped his forehead forward and rested on Jaime's thigh. "That was close."

"Wouldn't have been a bad thing." Jaime gripped the base of Oliver's shaft, holding it up, and swiped his flattened tongue from base to head. "I want you to coat my mouth." With the tip of his tongue, he traced the ridge of Oliver's glans. "But I'd like to suck some more first." With that explanation, he parted his lips and took Oliver in again.

Oliver's eyes shut as his jaw dropped open, the pleasure coursing through him nearly overwhelming. He drew in a gasping breath and because his lips were nearly touching Jaime's skin, with it came Jaime's flavor. One taste was an aphrodisiac, and it reminded Oliver that he could have more.

Forcing his eyes open, he parted his lips and slid them over Jaime's cock, flicking his tongue as he went. Beside him, Jaime moaned and Oliver wanted more of those sounds; he wanted to be the reason for those sounds. So, following Jaime's lead, he slid his mouth over Jaime's erection.

"Ungh," Jaime groaned around a mouthful of dick and sucked harder.

Oliver responded with his own indecipherable noise and clutched Jaime's ass, pulling him closer as he lowered his head. After that, the end was inevitable and Oliver welcomed it. With

Jaime's cock spreading his lips and precum slicking his tongue, he rocked his hips and pumped in and out of Jaime's eager mouth. He came first, yanking his head back with a shout as pleasure pulsed from him in wave after wave.

Jaime didn't miss a beat, swallowing down his seed and welcoming his pumps. Only when Oliver was completely spent, chest heaving and lungs burning, did Jaime pull his mouth away.

Oliver wanted to tell him he would finish his part just as soon as he could get oxygen into his brain, but Jaime tipped onto his back, fisted his own dick, and went to town, jerking at a rapid clip until his back arched and he shot, ejaculate streaking across his chest.

The scent of sex intensified, and before Oliver could think about what he was doing, he rolled onto all fours, crouched over Jaime, and licked up his tangy offering.

"Oh Christ." Jaime's big hand returned to the back of Oliver's head, petting him. "Don't let anyone tell you you're bad in bed, Oliver." He massaged his fingertips into Oliver's neck. "Seriously. Nobody. Ever."

Oliver lapped at Jaime's nipples and the base of this throat and then licked his way down his sternum, making sure to clean every drop of cum and sweat.

"Come here." Jaime curled his hands around Oliver's cheeks and pulled him forward until their lips met. "Mmm." He tugged on Oliver's lower lip with both of his and then slid his tongue into Oliver's mouth in a slow, sensual kiss.

Sated, Oliver lowered himself onto the mattress, and they turned toward each other, arms wrapping around one another as the kiss gentled.

"That was okay?" Oliver asked.

"It was much, much better than okay." Jaime rubbed the tip

of his nose against Oliver's.

Nodding, Oliver laid his head on Jaime's shoulder. He believed Jaime. Not just because he didn't think the other man would lie to him, but also because the intensity and pleasure couldn't have been one-sided. He snuggled closer and sighed contentedly.

After a few minutes, Jaime pulled the crumpled duvet out from underneath them and, keeping his arm around Oliver, managed to mostly cover them with the blanket.

"Comfortable?" he asked as he held Oliver close and rubbed his nape.

"Very." Jaime's muscular chest made a great pillow.

"Me too."

Oliver mapped Jaime's muscles with his fingertips, breathed in his scent, and thought about what he had just experienced. "It wasn't like this before."

He didn't need to give any more of an explanation for Jaime to understand his reference.

"You were nervous and he probably was too. But now you know that it's not a matter of not being able to do something."

"Uh-huh." Oliver walked his fingers around Jaime's areola and watched his nipple wrinkle into a hard pebble. "But I'm still not sure I could be like this with anyone else."

"Is that your way of saying you want to practice some more?" There was amusement in Jaime's voice.

"They say practice makes perfect, and I want to make sure I get it right," Oliver said, keeping his tone light. In truth, while he was still committed to learning how to be a good lover, he now also yearned for more time with Jaime. Getting attached to a man who saw him as a paycheck was, at best, silly, and at worst, reckless. But with Jaime's tender hands caressing his back and Jaime's warm lips brushing over his forehead, Oliver's heart didn't *feel* like he was nothing more than a job, and his brain, it seemed, had gone on vacation.

"You won't need to twist my elbow to get me to go along with that plan, but I need some downtime before my body can catch up to my mind and my libido. How about we take a cut scene and talk for a little while before we get back to it?"

The mention of time reminded Oliver that his was limited. He started to sit up, but Jaime put his hand on his shoulder, stopping him.

"We've been here about an hour."

"Oh, okay." They had two more hours. Oliver relaxed and went back to exploring Jaime's chest. "What do you want to talk about?"

"Tell me about your week."

"Nothing interesting to tell." Oliver shrugged. "It was good. I pretty much worked nonstop, but I like work so that's not a bad thing."

"It's great you enjoy your job, but making time for other things would help you accomplish some of those goals you've mentioned." He dug strong fingers into Oliver's shoulders, massaging him. "You told me you want to meet people."

"Yeah, I know. I do." Oliver sat up. The sex and massage had worked out his tension, but he rolled his shoulders out of habit. "But if I wasn't working, I'd be sitting alone in my apartment. I don't have friends here yet."

"You definitely won't make friends inside your apartment." Jaime scrunched his eyebrows and pressed his lips together, looking as if he was genuinely considering Oliver's situation. "Do you do things with people from work outside of the office?" Jaime squeezed Oliver's knee. "Maybe go for dinner or drinks when you're there late?"

"Not really." Oliver shook his head. "Everyone's nice, but stuff like that doesn't come up."

Jaime tilted his lips up at the corners and, keeping his voice low, said, "You could bring it up."

"I'm not like that, Jaime." Oliver ground his teeth together in frustration. "I wouldn't know what to say or do or—" He sighed. "If someone invites me to go along somewhere, I'll go, but I can't be the…instigator or whatever."

After a half-dozen beats of silence, Jaime said, "Let's go out. You and me."

"What?" Oliver blinked and stared at him.

"I'm inviting you to go out with me. Next weekend."

"I, uh… I don't understand."

"You'll see how much fun it can be to get out of the house and hang out."

"But…" Flustered, Oliver wasn't sure what to say. "I won't know anyone."

"You'll know me and maybe we'll meet new people and chat with them."

"I don't think that's a good idea." Oliver had never been good at meeting people, and he had no desire to try doing it in front of an audience. Even if the audience was Jaime.

"I know it's a good idea." Jaime rose, sat directly in front of Oliver, and took both of his hands in his own. "You hired me to help you do things differently in Seattle than you did in Oklahoma, right?"

"Sort of." Oliver's skin itched—a stress reaction he'd had since childhood—and he resented its appearance in the space he had thought would be safe. "I'm paying you to help me be different in bed."

"I'm good for more than sex," Jaime said, loosening his grip on Oliver's hands.

Damn, that was an epic fail. Oliver's insecurities and worries took a backseat as he rushed to fix the insult he had inadvertently lobbed. "I know. You're smart and nice and I totally hit the bonus round when I found your ad. I didn't mean—"

"Go out with me next weekend, Oliver. One hour, two hours tops, and then we can head to a hotel and have alone time."

"Okay." Oliver bobbed his head. At that moment, he would have agreed to just about anything to show Jaime he recognized his worth as more than what he did in bed.

"Awesome." Jaime beamed. "We're going to have fun." He leaned forward and kissed Oliver. "You'll see."

Chapter 6

"HEY, BABY BOY." Jaime squatted on the walnut parquet wood floor and scratched behind the light brown Chihuahua's perky ears. At fourteen, Rex no longer had boundless energy, but he still propped his front feet onto Jaime's bent knee and wriggled his backside with excitement. "I missed you too. Yes, I did."

"You're welcome here any time, Jaime," an amused voice said from behind him. "Especially with that greeting."

Looking back over his shoulder, Jaime grinned at his former boyfriend, now best friend. "Quit staring at my ass, perv."

"You can cut me off from touching, but if you're going to stick it out like that, I'm going to look."

"Whatever." Shaking his head, Jaime chuckled and returned his attention to the dog who was now crawling into his lap. "Come here, Rex. That's my boy." Keeping the dog in his arms, Jaime straightened.

"Where are Kiki and Lulu?" Jack asked.

"Searching your house for a rug to pee on." Jaime's dogs had rushed away the second they had walked into Jack's house. They were probably looking for the many treats and toys Jack kept on hand for Rex, but teasing Jack was fun.

"Not funny." Jack stepped closer, and they leaned toward each other, lips brushing. "Thanks for coming to stay with him again. I'll be back by Sunday afternoon."

"Happy to do it." Jaime gently ran his fingertips over Rex's white muzzle. "How's he doing?"

"He's okay. Getting older but still healthy."

"How about your mom?" Jaime looked into Jack's pale blue eyes.

"Older and not healthy." Jack dragged his fingers through his closely shorn blond hair and sighed. "I have a half hour before I need to leave for the airport." He began walking toward the kitchen. "Want a drink?"

"Sure." Jaime set Rex down, picked up his duffle bag, and followed Jack. "Is there anything I can be doing to help with your mom?"

"Staying here with Rex while I go visit her helps. I can't take him into the hospital. He'd be miserable at a boarding place. And he barks like a demon at every dog sitter I bring in here." Jack pulled the giant stainless steel refrigerator door open.

"Demon? Our sweet boy?" Jaime set his bag beside the island, crouched down, and petted Rex again. "Nooo. You're an angel, aren't you?"

"Only 'cause he loves you."

"The feeling's mutual." Jaime scratched Rex's chin and then turned when he heard a rush of tapping feet. "Rex, your friends are coming."

The older dog looked at Jaime pleadingly.

"Nothing to be done about it, bud. They're here for the weekend." Jaime laughed and stood up as his two smaller dogs skidded into the room and jumped on Rex. Sure enough, Kiki held a brown squeaky toy between her teeth while Lulu was biting down on a bone.

"At least they're keeping you young," Jack said to his dog as he handed Jaime a bottle of iced tea.

"He doesn't seem particularly grateful for that." Opening the bottle, Jaime looked at the label. Mango white tea. Jack hated mango but it was Jaime's favorite. "Thank you."

"I'm displacing you for the weekend. Least I could do."

Tipping the bottle against his lips, Jaime looked around. The nineteen twenties mansion had been meticulously returned to its original beauty. The ceilings soared to twenty feet in some areas. The kitchen gleamed with Italian marble countertops and stainless steel appliances. And the walls were covered in antique millwork.

"Staying at your place isn't a hardship." Jaime looked down at his dogs playing. Well, two of the dogs were his. Rex was technically Jack's dog even though Jaime had been beside him the day he'd adopted Rex from the rescue. "And you know I love spending time with my boy." Delaying the awkward conversation he needed to have, Jaime returned the bottle to his mouth and gulped down the rest of the tea.

"Want another one?"

"Sure." Jaime stepped over to the cabinet housing the trashcans, pulled it open, and dropped the bottle into the recycling bin. "I already had plans for tonight when you called." Jaime gripped the white countertops and looked out the window at Jack's perfectly manicured garden.

"A date?" Jack asked, a slight tremor in his voice.

Jaime dipped his chin twice.

"Is it serious?"

"No, but…" Jaime thought about Oliver Barnaby. "I think it can be if…" Knowing Jack, he'd find the story of how Jaime met Oliver funny. But Jaime hoped to transition his liaisons with Oliver out of hidden hotel rooms and into real life, and the shy younger man would be mortified if anyone knew those types of details about his personal life, so Jaime kept the information to himself.

"If?" Jack prompted.

"It feels a little weird talking about this with you." Jaime turned around and leaned his butt against the counter.

"We broke up a lifetime ago."

Eight years wasn't a lifetime, but when Jaime thought back to who he had been at age thirty-two, he could see Jack's point.

Continuing to speak, Jack said, "And we've both dated plenty of people over the years." He paused and scrunched his eyebrows together. "So if you're uncomfortable talking to me about this one, he's different." Jack walked through the long kitchen, pulled out a chair next to the round antique table facing the bay window, and sat down. "It's already serious."

"We've texted a lot." Multiple times a day. "But tonight'll only be our fourth time actually seeing each other." He left out the fact that the previous three times had been in a bed.

"That's not an answer."

Sighing, Jaime stepped away from the counter and joined Jack at the table. "I really like him. He's somebody I can see myself with." Jaime rolled the iced tea bottle between his hands and then raised his gaze to meet Jack's. "Long term."

Not skipping a beat, Jack said, "I'm happy for you."

Jaime arched his eyebrows.

"I mean it." Jack curled his hand around Jaime's forearm. "Our decision to end it was mutual, and I've been under no delusions that anything would change. I'm not the right guy for you." Jack looked away and swallowed hard, his Adam's apple bobbing. "I understand that."

"Sometimes I wish you could have been." Jaime slid his arm down until his hand met Jack's.

"Sometimes I wish the same thing." Jack twined their fingers together. After a few minutes of silence, he said, "Are you planning on having him stay here with you this weekend?"

"Would you mind if I did?"

"It's fine." Jack released Jaime's hand and cracked his knuckles. "You sleep in a guest room, not in my bed."

"It's your home, Jack. I don't need to bring another man here if it makes you uncomfortable."

"You already had the date scheduled."

"A date doesn't have to mean a sleepover." Jaime fiddled with the cap on his bottle.

Jack nodded and rubbed his lips together. "You can have him stay here with you, Jaime. Eight years is long enough."

"For you too?"

After a brief hesitation, Jack nodded. "For me too." He took a deep breath and released it. "It's time we both found someone we can settle down with."

"Are you saying we're old?" Jaime joked, hoping to lighten the mood.

"Not me. Only you."

"That's some trick considering you were born two years before me."

"Age is a state of mind." Jack grinned and tapped his finger against his temple.

"Then I'm upping that two years to twenty." Jaime raised both hands in the air and pantomimed shooting a basketball. "Swoosh. All net."

"Nicely played." Jack chuckled.

"You get the assist." Jaime picked up his tea and took a sip.

Flicking his gaze away, Jack quietly said, "Want to tell me about him?"

Jaime set the bottle down. "If it goes anywhere, I'll do you one better and introduce the two of you."

"*If?*" Jack shook his head. "I have yet to meet someone who can resist the James Snow charm. If you've set your sights on this guy, the word is *when.*"

WHEN JAIME AND his ex had separated and sold their house eight years earlier, Jack had decided to stay in Capitol Hill, so Jaime, wanting to give each of them space, found a place twenty minutes away in Laurelhurst. As much as he loved his view of Lake Washington and the quiet tranquility in his neighborhood, Capitol Hill was still his favorite place to socialize, which was the reason he had chosen the Madison Pub for his night out with Oliver.

Instead of driving to the bar, Jaime left his car in Jack's garage and got an Uber. That way he wouldn't have to deal with parking, and if Oliver brought his own car, they could leave together and he could warm the cold feet he expected Oliver to get once he suggested they go to a house for the entire night instead of a hotel for an hour or two. Aside from calming Oliver's nerves, Jaime would have to find a way to work around Oliver's finance-based time constraints. Even the reduced fifty-dollar hourly rate would add up to more than Oliver could afford if he stayed with Jaime for the night and maybe even the weekend.

But Jaime needed to spend more than a few hours at a clip with Oliver to have any hope of getting him comfortable with the idea of having an actual relationship. Mulling over his options, Jaime looked out the window and enjoyed the transition from beautiful estates with pristine lawns to upscale coffee shops and apartments, to office buildings and dive restaurants. When the ten-minute drive ended, he was no closer to a decision on how to handle his unusual situation. Stepping out of the car, he breathed in the night air and told himself that, by the time they left the bar, he would think of some way to get Oliver to go along with his plan of spending the night, and hopefully the next day, together.

Cars were parked bumper to bumper on the street directly in front of the Madison Pub, so Jaime had the Uber driver drop him at the end of the street. It was a few minutes shy of seven, which meant Jaime was early, but he wasn't surprised to see Oliver leaning against the red brick building next to the bar, hunched over his phone. After only a month knowing Oliver, Jaime had already figured out that the sexy man took punctuality seriously.

"You're early," he said as he approached.

Jerking his head up, Oliver looked around and then spotted Jaime. "I wasn't sure how long it'd take to get here and I didn't want to be late." He pushed the phone against his jean pocket, didn't manage to get it in, fiddled with it, and eventually looked down and got the phone into his pocket.

"You're very considerate." As soon as he was close enough, Jaime curled his palm around the back of Oliver's neck and massaged it. "And nervous?"

"A little," Oliver admitted, ducking his chin. "I've never been here." He wiped his palms on the front of his jeans and tilted his head up toward the red letters spelling the bar's name. "Does pub mean it's a British theme?"

"I think I've seen a few Irish decorations, but really, it's just a casual bar. Pool tables, darts, and TVs." He slid his hand to Oliver's shoulder and squeezed it. "They get a friendly crowd here. Once you meet them, you'll feel better."

"I get nervous about going out with people I know. I'm not sure why you think I'll do any better with strangers," Oliver snapped. He immediately widened his eyes and then bit his lip. "Sorry. That was rude."

It wasn't really, and even if it had been, Oliver's apology came so quickly nobody could have been offended by it. That soft-hearted sensitivity enchanted Jaime.

"No worries about the snark. I've heard worse." Jaime rubbed Oliver's back soothingly. "And I'm here. You're not nervous with me, right?"

"It's different with you."

Jaime wanted to believe the difference wasn't because Oliver was paying him. The exchange of money obviously gave Oliver a none-too-small measure of comfort, especially the first night they'd met. But while their arrangement had an undisputable sexual component, the sex wasn't the main focus. At least not to Jaime.

The insecurities and desires Oliver had shared with him were more intimate and frank than what he'd heard from guys he'd dated for months, let alone one-night stands. Jaime focused on those insights as they walked into the bar. Oliver had said more than once that he wanted to be more social in Seattle, that he wanted to make friends. So Jaime disregarded Oliver's body language and expression, both of which belonged on a man walking into a place where he would be fired or jailed or attacked, lowered his arm to Oliver's back, and led them toward the door.

"Let's give it a go for half an hour, okay?" He had planned the night with a goal of making Oliver feel good, not torturing him. "We'll have a beer, play a game or two, and if you're not having fun we can leave," he said, hoping to make Oliver feel better.

"I can do a half hour." Oliver raised his lips up in what looked like an effort at a smile and walked beside him.

As they neared the door, music and laughter spilled from the bar and an employee standing by the entrance waved them in. "All our Deschutes pints are five bucks a pop tonight, guys. Have a good time." They stepped into the large, dimly lit space, and as Oliver flicked his gaze around, tension bled from his stiff back.

"Is that pinball?" Oliver squinted at the row of brightly colored machines lining one wall.

"It sure is. You like to play?" Jaime started walking toward the machines, keeping his hand on Oliver's lower back as they wove through the other bar patrons.

"I don't do it much anymore, but when I was a kid, my parents took my sister and me to this swimming complex every weekend in the summer. They had a snack bar with pinball machines and I spent hours perfecting my game." Oliver smiled at the memory. "Made my parents a little nuts because I was supposed to be swimming, but I've never had a build for a bathing suit."

"Hey." Jaime stepped in front of Oliver and turned to face him. "I like your body. I like it in clothes and out of clothes."

"I was making a joke."

Given the number of times Oliver had made disparaging remarks about his own weight, Jaime sensed there was more than harmless humor behind the comment. Rather than pushing the issue or arguing about it, he leaned down until his mouth was right beside Oliver's ear and whispered, "I would love to spend a day at a pool with you, checking you out."

Oliver's breath stuttered. "You're not allowed to, uh, rev me up in public."

"I'm sure you wouldn't be the only guy here in that condition." Jaime moved his right leg forward, brushing his thigh against Oliver's groin.

"I thought we were going to play pinball?" Oliver rasped.

"Lead the way." Jaime stepped aside and nudged Oliver forward. "I'll walk behind you so I can check out your ass."

That comment had Oliver laughing. "You're silly." He looked back over his shoulder, narrowed his eyes, and painted his face with an expression Jaime assumed was supposed to be menacing. "I almost feel bad about the painful humiliation I'm about to inflict on you."

Hearing Oliver's confidence reinvigorated Jaime's good mood. "Big talker," he said with a chuckle. "Let's see if you can bring the action."

Forty minutes later, Jaime was leaning against the wall next to a pinball machine and popping mixed nuts into his mouth. "Is your strategy to beat me by hogging the machine until last call?"

"I'm still on my first game." Oliver clicked the left flipper button, and the ball banged its way up the machine, creating flickering lights and excited noises before it hit a ball that was lodged along the right side of the machine.

"You've tried to get that ball out a thousand times. I think it's stuck."

"It's a captive ball. I'm not trying to get it out. Knocking it into targets gets me points." When the ball rolled back down, Oliver clicked the button and caught and held the ball on a flipper. He then turned his head toward Jaime and narrowed his eyes. "Are you hustling me?"

Jaime arched his eyebrows, raised one corner of his lips, and gave him a pointed look.

Drawing in a quick breath, Oliver hissed, "Not that kind of hustling." The bar was too dark for a visual confirmation, but Jaime was sure the man was blushing. "I mean the one where you pretend to be clueless but you're really a pro."

"Hustler. Pro." Jaime popped a nut into his mouth. "I'm sensing a theme here."

Oliver's hand slipped, causing the flipper to move down and the ball to roll off. When Oliver noticed what was happening, he tilted the machine but it was too late to stop the ball from falling into the drain.

"You distracted me on purpose!"

"I really didn't." Jaime chuckled. "You set up a perfect teasing opportunity and I couldn't pass it up. Ending your reign of terror was just a happy coincidence." He pushed his shoulder off the wall and set the folded paper holding the nuts on the tall table beside them. "The rest of those are yours." He shoved the sleeves on his black cotton sweater up to his elbows. "It's finally my turn."

"That's a negative." Oliver pulled the plunger and another ball sprung into the game. "I earned an extra ball." He pressed the flipper button and sent the ball sailing. "And now that I'm on to your shenanigans, you're not going to topple my focus." The ball hit a red and black target and all the lights flashed at once. "Bam! Bonus!"

"Oh for goodness sake." Jaime sighed dramatically, picked up the nuts, and returned to his spot on the wall. "At this rate, I'm never going to play."

"Ignoring you."

"At least I have these nuts to keep me company." He ate an almond.

Oliver coughed.

"Although I have to say, I liked them better when they were fresh from the heat lamp." He waited for the ball to roll down and then leaned close enough for his dick to rub against Oliver's ass and his breath to tickle Oliver's ear and said, "But you already know how much I enjoy warm nuts in my mouth, don't you?"

Trembling, Oliver's eyes slid shut and he groaned. The ball rolled into the drain.

"That's game," Jaime whispered.

Oliver blinked his eyes open and, voice sounding strained, said, "You suck."

"I like doing that too." Jaime grinned.

"It's your turn."

"We've passed our half-hour limit. I don't mind skipping my turn if you want to leave."

"Oh, uh, no. That's okay." Oliver shook his head. "We're not done with pinball. You're up."

"Okay, but after this, we're getting a drink." Jaime shuffled to the front of the machine and muttered, "We're in a bar and I can't find my way to a beer."

"Poor baby." Oliver did not sound at all sympathetic. "The thirst must be killing you."

"Hey, you know how it is when you've had nuts in your mouth all night. They're salty."

Oliver rolled his eyes. "Less talking, more playing."

"Fine." Jaime handed the paper cone to Oliver. "I'm sure this won't take long."

"Not if those ridiculous comments and questions you've been spouting were on the up and up."

"I have no idea what you're talking about." Jaime pulled the plunger and watched a ball bump up and then roll down into the drain. "Oops."

"That was painful. Truly."

"What was it you said to me?" Jaime reached for the plunger again. "Oh yeah. Ignoring you."

Beside him, Oliver laughed. "Just don't ignore the flippers this time. They're a key part of the game."

Jaime released the plunger and gently nudged the machine, sending the ball through a series of obstacles up the right side.

"I don't think I've ever seen a ball move like that without hitting a single target."

After curving around the top, the ball started rolling down the left side.

"Remember to use the flippers this time," Oliver said.

Jaime didn't move.

"Jaime! The flippers."

"Oh right." Jaime twisted his head to look at Oliver and, using his most innocent voice said, "Like this?" He simultaneously pressed the buttons on both sides of the machine, sending both flippers up and leaving the widest possible opening for the ball.

"No, you…"

The ball smoothly rolled into the drain.

"You can't be this bad! Nobody is this bad." Oliver shook his head. "You're either the worst player alive or the best one, because that was so bad it had to have taken effort."

"You said to use the flippers. I used the flippers. I was following your directions, so if anything, that means you're bad."

"I have the high score on this game." Oliver pointed to the display where red lights showed his point total. "You, on the other hand, have zero points and one ball left." He pointed to the current game's score. "The problem is most definitely not me."

"Maybe I'm lulling you into a sense of complacency."

"Why would you do that when this is the last game?"

"I must be a horrible strategist."

Oliver narrowed his eyes, and Jaime curled his lips over his teeth to stop himself from smiling. "Last ball." He spread his legs, moved his left foot slightly forward, curled his left hand around the side of the machine, and pulled the plunger with his right one. The ball shot up, hitting certain targets before coming back down. Jaime caught it on a flipper and sent it back up to hit a different set of targets.

"Are you…"

Oliver stepped closer, but Jaime kept his focus on the game. After another trip up, bouncing from target to target, the ball came down. Jaime tilted the machine and raised the flipper, knocking the ball against three targets in succession. The lights flashed and music played.

"You got a jackpot!" Oliver shouted excitedly.

Turning toward him, Jaime said, "Is that good?"

"Good! You just hit all those sequences in order. It's amazing." His eyes widened. "Watch the ball. Jaime, the ball!"

Jaime took his time to turn back toward the game. "Oops," he said as the ball slid down the drain. "Guess that's game."

Jaw open, Oliver looked from Jaime to the pinball machine and back again. "You did that on purpose."

"Did what on purpose?" He walked toward the bar.

"The whole thing!"

"You're saying I lost on purpose? Why would I do that?" He was having the best time.

"I have no idea. But the way you didn't get a single point

with the first two balls was so unnatural. There is no way someone could do it on accident twice in a row. And the jackpot had like five different combination shots you hit in sequence. Are you telling me you weren't trying to do that?"

"Let's say I was trying." They reached the bar, and Jaime propped his hip against it and crossed his arms over his chest. "Does that mean I won even though you had the higher score?"

"High*est* score," Oliver corrected. "And no way."

"Okay." Jaime shrugged, turned around, and waved to get the bartender's attention.

"What does that mean?"

"It's the universal signal for, 'Hey, barkeep, pour me a drink.'"

"I'm talking about the game."

"What game?" Thank goodness Jaime had his back to Oliver because he couldn't keep the smile off his face.

"There's a mirror above the bar, smart guy." Oliver's full, warm body pressed against Jaime's back. "I can see you laughing."

Jaime flicked his gaze up. There was a gap in the glasses stacked in front of the mirror and, sure enough, it was located in the perfect spot to reflect his face. "Oops."

"You were playing me!"

Grinning, Jaime turned around and held his thumb and pointer finger an inch apart. "Just a little."

"Why?"

"Because playing with you is fun."

"It's fun for me too." Oliver narrowed his eyes. "And I won the game."

"I like this competitive side of your personality." Jaime curled his hand around Oliver's hip and tugged him forward.

"It's sexy."

"Quit changing the subject," Oliver said, his voice huskier.

"I intentionally missed the targets a couple of times, and I nailed the jackpot sequence once. You had forty minutes of nearly perfect play with a few bonuses of your own. You won the game."

"Don't humor me."

"I'm not."

"You know what? Fine," Oliver huffed, planting his hands on his waist. "We'll get the beer and then we're playing another round. No funny business this time."

"I thought you liked having funny business with me." Jaime pretend-pouted.

"That expression looks ridiculous on a man your age and I'm serious. Play to win this time."

"You want to learn some tricks from me?"

"I want to make sure my bragging rights are indisputable and ironclad."

"Ouch." Jaime put his palm over his heart. "So cold."

"Uh-huh. Whatever." Oliver jerked his gaze from one side of the bar to the other. "Where's that bartender?"

"All that teasing and you're desperate for a drink too."

"I'm desperate to beat you at pinball. The drink's necessary to pull you away from the bar and back to the machine."

"Likely excuse." Mindful of the mirror, Jaime kept his expression neutral as he turned back around and flagged down the bartender.

Their agreed upon half hour at the bar had already turned into an hour and yet Oliver wanted to stay even later. The night was a success.

Chapter 7

"HERE YOU GO." Jaime held a highball glass out to Oliver. "Thanks." Uncurling his fingers from a clenched fist, Oliver reached for the drink and then took a sip.

"How's it taste?" Jaime plopped down beside him on Jack's living room couch.

"Like citrus and gin." He looked around the room and then lowered his gaze and mumbled, "Along with a dash of every bad decision I've ever made."

"Good thing I left out the regret aftertaste."

Oliver's cheeks reddened. "I didn't mean to say that out loud." He sighed. "I guess I'm just nervous." He swallowed more of his drink. "This is really good."

"It's a fuzzy navel. That's orange juice and schnapps, which is pretty much peach-flavored gin. You have a refined palate."

"It's a learned skill. I keep it exposed to all available flavors on a regular basis." Oliver smiled as he spoke and then took another drink. "Being a good eater is my superpower."

Unlike the previous comments he had made about his own weight, which seemed like attempts to talk himself down before anyone could beat him to it, Oliver sounded happy and that made Jaime happy.

"I like that about you." Jaime curled his palm around the top of Oliver's thigh.

"That I'm a good eater?"

"I haven't had the pleasure of your company over dinner yet, but yes." Jaime nodded. "Guys who count every calorie and obsess about their pants size and try every new diet craze just… It's a turn off for me." It was more than those actions though. Jaime tried to think of the right words to explain why he was attracted to heavier men. "When I told you that not every guy wants someone with a gym body"—he met Oliver's gaze—"I was speaking from personal experience. It took me a long time to figure that out." A long time and the end of a relationship that, on paper, should have been perfect. But no matter how much he respected Jack's intelligence, admired his business acumen, and enjoyed his company, he couldn't create a spark when there wasn't any heat, and he couldn't keep pretending his feelings for his ex were romantic. Taking a deep breath, he raised his glass to his lips. "Anyway, I like your superpower."

Oliver lowered his gaze, but his lips were turned up in a smile. They sat in silence for a few moments, both of them nursing their drinks, and then Oliver quietly said, "I'm glad I'm here."

Jaime beamed. "I'm glad you're here too." Every moment he spent with Oliver made Jaime want to be with him more and now he had him for the entire night. Maybe the weekend.

"I didn't want to say goodbye when we left the bar, but—" Oliver put his glass on his knee and twisted it from left to right, took a deep breath, and looked at Jaime from underneath his lashes. "You're sure being with you all night is okay even though I only paid the regular rate?"

After a great night drinking, talking, and laughing at the Madison Pub, Jaime had fabricated an excuse for Oliver to come home with him—something about wanting company when he was staying in a strange house. He wasn't sure it would work, but Oliver had agreed without much of a fuss. And then he had taken out his wallet and handed Jaime a hundred and fifty dollars—three hours at the half-off rate Jaime had tossed out the first night they met.

Like he had every other time Oliver handed him money, Jaime had wanted to shove it back, but he had held his instincts in check, said thank you, and folded the bills into his wallet. Oliver still needed the self-created crutch he got from their financial exchange, so if Jaime wanted to build a relationship with him, he would have to go along with it until Oliver recognized his non-monetary value. Something he would ensure happened soon. Very soon.

"Absolutely. You're doing me a favor by keeping me company." Jaime tickled his fingertips over the back of Oliver's hand. "If anything I should be the one paying you."

"Yeah right." Oliver snorted. He pressed the glass to his lips and looked up at the coffered ceiling. "This is a nice house." He moved his gaze to the intricate millwork on the walls. "Really nice."

"Yes, it is."

Returning his focus to Jaime, he said, "You're dog sitting for the owner?"

"Mmm-hmm. Rex, that's the biggest of the pups you met, is really finicky about who stays with him." Happily buzzed from the drinks and the conversation, Jaime raised his glass to his lips and relaxed into the sofa. At least he tried to relax. Instead his back hit what felt like a block of wood and he tipped to the side. "What the…" He righted himself and looked over his shoulder. "This is the most uncomfortable couch ever." He poked the taut cloth behind him, his fingers barely making a dent. "Why would they make it so stiff?"

"Probably to avoid scrunched up fabric or misshaped cushions," Oliver said.

Glancing down to where the top of the sofa connected with the bottom of his ribcage, Jaime added, "And so short?"

"I think it's made to look good, not feel good." Perched on the end of Jack's sofa, he fidgeted with his now empty glass. "You could ask your client why he chose it?" he suggested hesitantly.

"Client?"

"The man who lives here?"

"Oh. Jack." Jaime reached for some throw pillows. "He redecorated this room not too long ago. Hired a designer"—he stuffed a pillow behind his back—"who apparently values appearance over comfort. Christ, even this pillow is stiff." Holding another pillow toward Oliver, he asked, "Want an unpillowy pillow?"

"Sure." Oliver leaned forward to make room for the pillow and fidgeted with his waistband.

"Take your jeans off if they're bothering you." Jaime drained his drink, set his glass on the round teak end table, and then pushed himself to his feet, grunting. "Actually, that's a good idea." He reached for his belt buckle.

"You're stripping?" Oliver jerked his gaze around in a panic. "Right here in the open?"

His hands on his belt, Jaime froze. "I was going to take my jeans off, but if it's stripping you want…" He looked around and spotted his phone on the kitchen counter, next to the bottle of schnapps. "I'll get the music."

"I didn't… I wasn't…" Oliver seemed unable to complete a sentence.

Jaime already knew him well enough to recognize that meant

he was either nervous or turned-on. In this case, it was probably a bit of both.

"Nobody else is here," he assured Oliver as he walked over to the large window facing the couch, phone now in hand. "And I'll close the curtains." He pulled the heavy silk brocade drapes. "See? Complete privacy." He scrolled through his music, said "This should work," and clicked on his exercise playlist. The first of a string of fast-paced songs started playing. "Hope you like Britney." After turning the volume up, he set the phone on the end table next to his glass, and stepped in front of the curtains.

Oliver stared at him, mouth open, eyes wide, and chest heaving. Nervous had completely transitioned to aroused.

Pride over his success and a liberal amount of alcohol flowing through Jaime's veins made him confident in his abilities, so with no hesitation, he began swinging his hips in time with the upbeat music thumping through the room. Trying to remember every stage dancer and music video he had ever seen, he replaced the left to right swings with front to back motions, turned around, and then he squatted until his ass nearly touched the wood floor before slowly rising again.

Behind him, Oliver gasped and, wanting to see his face, Jaime flipped around, one hand cupped behind his head and the other trailing down his chest to his zipper. His initial plan had been to take off his jeans, but now that he was removing clothing with a purpose other than comfort, he reconsidered. Bare legs, briefs, and a sweater wouldn't look as sexy as shirtless wearing jeans, and Jaime was definitely going for sexy. He wanted Oliver so worked up that desire and need overtook him and left no room in his mind for his hesitations, anxieties, and insecurities.

With Oliver's brown eyes glued to him, Jaime walked his fingers to the bottom of his sweater, curled them around the hem, and pulled up. Inch by inch, he exposed his stomach and chest, all while continuing to swing his hips in time with the music. When the swath of fabric passed his nipples, his movements stuttered. Was there a way to look hot while pulling a shirt over his head? He couldn't think of an example, his mind instead filling with images of guys yanking off flimsy Velcro-connected shirts. He wasn't going to suddenly turn Hulk and gain the strength to tear off a cotton sweater, so he made the best of the situation and hurriedly pulled it over his head and then tossed it aside.

When he refocused on Oliver, he saw wide eyes, flared nostrils, and an open mouth. From the first night they had been together, he had noticed Oliver's sensuality. Touch during sex was a given, but Oliver engaged other senses. He seemed to genuinely enjoy smelling every part of Jaime's body, burying his face in Jaime's armpit or groin and breathing in deeply. His need to inhale scents was often followed by a desire to taste, his tongue swiping over sweat-slick skin as if it was a delicacy. Never before had Jaime felt as sexy as he did reflected in Oliver's eyes.

With his chest bare, Jaime danced his way to the couch and flicked open the button on his jeans. He was close enough to hear Oliver gasp and moan, and the sounds of arousal from the man who had taken over his every fantasy pushed him to keep moving forward. Hands pinching his own nipples, he straddled Oliver's legs and thrust his hips, rubbing his groin against Oliver's face.

"Oh God." Oliver gasped, and his eyes widened farther as his nose twitched. "Oh God. Can I… I want to…"

Answering without words, Jaime stayed in place, his fingers locked behind his head and his erection bulging against his jeans as he rolled his hips and gyrated a hair's distance from Oliver's gorgeous face.

Happy with the non-verbal approval, Oliver raised his hands to Jaime's chest and reverently glided them over his heated skin. "You feel so good," he rasped, voice rough. "Always feel so good." He pushed forward, getting closer to the front of Jaime's jeans. "And you smell... Oh God."

With anyone else, Jaime may have held himself slightly back, leaving space between his balls and someone's face. After all, he had been in tight jeans in a warm bar all night. Nothing about him was shower fresh, especially his package. But Oliver's reactions so far showed that bottled scents weren't what enticed the man, so instead of keeping air between them, Jaime yanked his zipper open, tangled his hand in the back of Oliver's hair, and pulled him against his briefs.

"Mmm." Oliver moaned and immediately clutched Jaime's hips. "Yes." He rubbed his face against Jaime's underwear, as if trying to cover himself in Jaime's scent. "So good."

If he had been ten years younger, the sheer eroticism of that act combined with the small bit of friction would have been enough to set Jaime off. Even at forty, his balls rose and his cock pulsed with need.

"You like that?" Jaime tightened his grip in Oliver's hair and rocked against him.

"So much." Rather than pulling away, Oliver pressed closer, his hot, moist breath soaking through the fabric of Jaime's briefs and giving him another layer of sensation.

"I want to pull down my underwear and come on your face." Not usually one for dirty talk or roughness in bed, Jaime's own words surprised him.

Oliver, on the other hand, didn't skip a beat. "Do it," he begged, desire-filled eyes gazing up at Jaime. "I want it."

"Not done dancing yet." Stepping away from Oliver's heat and touch was an exercise in torture, but Jaime wanted something different tonight so he forced himself to move. When Oliver whimpered, Jaime almost changed his mind, but he managed to satisfy himself by caressing Oliver's cheek and whispering, "Soon."

Falling back into the rhythm of the music wasn't as easy with his dick as hard as stone and his balls aching for release, but Jaime swayed and squatted, touching himself as he slowly worked his jeans off.

"You're so beautiful," Oliver whispered, his eyes raking over Jaime's form and spending extra time on his groin.

"How about from this angle?" Jaime turned around, hands laced together behind his neck to highlight the muscles in his back and the breadth of his shoulders. "Or this one?" He caressed his flanks as he widened his stance and then he bent over, pushing his ass up and out. "Do you like this?" Looking over his shoulder, he watched Oliver's expression as he skated his palm over one muscular globe.

Head bobbing, Oliver opened his mouth but no sound came out.

"Want a closer look?" Knowing Oliver was too far gone to respond, Jaime continued with his teasing dance, pulling his underwear down his legs and then stepping out of them. Body swaying, he returned to his spot straddling Oliver's legs, but this time rather than facing him, he left his back to Oliver. And then, keeping his legs straight, he bent in half.

The sound Oliver made was a mix of a shocked gasp, a pained whimper, and an excited moan. His soft, thick fingers made contact with Jaime's back, hips, and butt, touching and exploring while his hot breath brushed across Jaime's skin.

Wanting to know how far his shy, inexperienced guy would take things when he had complete control, Jaime held himself still. Soft lips and a wet tongue soon brushed across his lower back and trailed down to his upper thigh. Trembling fingers gripped both sides of his cheeks and spread him open. Cool air from the room twined with hot gusts of breath. And then Oliver's tongue tickled his cleft. The first touch was light, hesitant, but it wasn't long before Oliver's grip tightened and his timid flicks transitioned to firm swipes. From above his balls, over his pucker, to the top of his cleft and back again, Oliver licked and moaned as he ate Jaime out with gusto.

"Feels amazing." A few strokes would be all he'd need to find sweet release, and his fingers itched to take himself in hand. But that pleasure would be so much better if it was accompanied by a stretched hole and a massaged prostate. "We should stop," he said breathlessly as he straightened.

"Why?" Oliver's skin was flush, his hair disheveled, and lips and chin glistened with saliva. He looked like he had been doing exactly what he had just been doing, and seeing the visual evidence of how much he had enjoyed focusing on Jaime, aroused him further. "Was I doing it wrong?"

He thought he was being clear with Oliver but his assurances weren't registering. He wondered if the problem was Oliver's self-esteem or his belief that Jaime's words were part of his rent-boy script. He wanted to tell Oliver that, for his part, the time they spent together had nothing to do with money. But staying in Oliver's life meant playing by his rules, and making a judgement about whether those rules had changed wasn't a job to tackle at midnight with his brain fuzzy from alcohol. So instead of speaking, Jaime leaned forward until his lips met Oliver's.

"Just the opposite. You do everything right." He caressed

Oliver's cheek. "You do it for me." He straddled Oliver's thighs, settled his ass over Oliver's cock, and began rocking. "I stopped because I want you to fuck me tonight." Desire flooded Oliver's eyes and with their torsos pressed together, Jaime could feel his heart banging. "Do you want to fuck me?"

Nostrils flared and fingers clutching Jaime's bare thighs, Oliver gulped and said, "Don't move for a minute, okay? I'm so close." He dropped his forehead against Jaime's chest and sucked in air. "Everything about you is amazing. The way you smell and the way you taste and the way you dance and... God, you work me up."

"You do the same thing to me." Jaime bucked his hips, pressing his erection against Oliver's stomach. "Can you feel that?"

"Not helping," Oliver bit out.

"What if I want you to come?"

"But you said—"

"Based on how revved up you are right now, I'm thinking you'll shoot the second you get inside. Am I right?"

"Doubt it'll take that long," Oliver admitted.

Jaime smiled. "Then how about we get one out of the way first?" He snuck his hands between them, reaching for Oliver's pants button.

Oliver immediately stiffened.

"What's wrong?"

"Nothing."

Jaime arched his eyebrows.

After a few moments of silence, Oliver sighed and quietly said, "I wish my body was like yours."

"I don't."

Oliver blinked in surprise.

"I mean it. I like your body."

"Even though you're pressed up against blubber and you

have to push my gut out of the way to reach my dick?"

"What do I need to say or do to make you believe I'm attracted to you?" Jaime lifted his hands, rubbed his palms against his eyes, and then cupped Oliver's cheeks. "You're funny and giving and really sweet." He slid his fingertips into the sides of Oliver's hair and tipped his head back until their eyes met. "But I'll be really frank with you, Oliver, if that was all there was to you, I wouldn't be here right now."

Oliver's breath seemed to stop.

"It took me a lot of years to figure out what does it for me, and I'm past the point in my life where I'm willing to pretend." Making sure he held Oliver's attention, he slowly lowered his hands, unfastened Oliver's pants, and reached into his boxers. "I *love* your body." He wrapped his fingers around Oliver's erection and started stroking. "I love pressing myself against you." He moved his fist up and down, not quickly but not slowly either. "Your thick thighs, your full ass, and yes, your round stomach, all make me insanely hot."

Oliver moaned and Jaime tightened the grip on his dick a fraction. "I want you to come in my hand right now, and then I want to get into bed with you and feel your big body on top of mine while you fuck me into the mattress."

"Jaime," Oliver rasped and clutched Jaime's waist. His chest heaved and his breaths came in fast, sharp gasps.

"Look at how beautiful you are." Jaime stared at Oliver's face—smooth skin, straight nose, round cheeks, and chocolate eyes. He curled his free hand around Oliver's cheek, dipped his head until their lips touched, and whispered, "I'm so glad I met you."

"Ah!" Oliver groaned. "Ah!"

Warm liquid flowed over Jaime's fist. "There it is." He smiled against Oliver's mouth and continued stroking. "Even more gorgeous when you come."

Oliver's chest heaved, his lips trembled, and his eyes glistened, making him look young and vulnerable.

"Shh. I'm here." Jaime held his chin with his thumb and pointer finger and leaned in for a kiss, this one sweet and gentle, calming. When Oliver's breathing eventually slowed and Jaime could no longer feel Oliver's heart pounding against his chest, he swiped his tongue from the bottom of Oliver's lips to the top and slowly leaned back. "You okay?"

"Yeah." Oliver swallowed. "That was…"

"I get it." He brushed his lips against Oliver's cheek, climbed off his lap, and reached his clean hand out. "Let's go to bed."

"Jaime?" Oliver placed his hand on Jaime's and stood.

"Yes?"

"Is this… Are we…" He bit his lip, flicked his gaze away, and shook his head. "Never mind."

Sensing an opening to the conversation he wanted to have anyway, Jaime moved close enough that there was no distance between them. "Tell me what you were going to say."

"I forgot."

He could press the issue and probably get Oliver to talk, but he noticed Oliver's shoulders rise, saw veins in the side of his neck pulse, and didn't miss the fact that the man refused to make eye contact with him. That tension didn't exist when Oliver was dealing with Jaime the escort and tense wasn't conducive to his plans for the night.

"Okay." Jaime moved their joined hands to his groin and pressed Oliver's palm against his erection. "Ready to help me with this?"

Desperate need replaced anxiety with flattering speed. "God yes."

Chapter 8

"I CAN'T BELIEVE you went outside like that," Oliver said when Jaime walked into the guest room.

"The dogs are too scared to go out alone in the dark." He hunkered down, straightened the two dog beds in the corner, and scratched Rex's head once he lay down. Normally Kiki and Lulu wrestled before falling asleep, but he had woken them to take them out, so they hopped onto their joint bed, curled together, and closed their eyes. "They'll use the dog door during the day, but if I don't take them out before bed, I risk waking up to presents in the morning."

"The going outside part I understand." Oliver dragged his gaze over Jaime's body. "But you're naked."

"I wasn't wearing anything, remember?" Jaime grinned as he lifted the duvet and climbed into bed beside Oliver. "And I didn't think getting dressed would make sense given our plans for the rest of the night." He paused and tilted his head to the side. "Unless you're into kinky costumes?"

Oliver fell into a coughing fit.

"I was kidding." Jaime laughed quietly. Oliver lay on his back, so Jaime settled on his side and scooted close enough that they touched from chest to thighs. "You don't strike me as the role-playing type."

"Are you?"

"Nope." Jaime shook his head and flattened his palm on

Oliver's chest. "I'm the boring middle-aged type."

"You're not boring," Oliver immediately said. Then he furrowed his brow. "What does that mean?"

"What does the boring middle-aged type mean?"

"Uh-huh."

"It means the only games I like to play come in cardboard boxes or digital format." Jaime slid his hand from Oliver's chest to his belly, enjoying the feeling of soft skin and silky hair. "How about you? Are you into bedroom games?"

"Me?" Oliver asked in surprise. "You know I don't have any experience."

"What about in your head?" He lightly tapped Oliver's temple with his forehead. "You're twenty-eight years old and single. I know you have fantasies."

The low light streaming from the bedside lamp illuminated Oliver's reddening face.

"Not really." Oliver wriggled self-consciously.

"Please don't try telling me you don't watch porn because I will not buy that line," Jaime teased.

"Porn isn't a fantasy."

"No?" Jaime asked curiously.

Oliver shook his head. "I, uh, sometimes like to click on certain sites when I masturbate but fantasies are something else."

Enjoying the conversation, Jaime reached for a pillow, fluffed it, and tucked it under his head. "How so?" He flung his calf over Oliver's legs and pressed his groin to Oliver's hip.

"I don't know." Oliver shrugged. "A fantasy is like a dream sequence, right? Even if it's a sexual one, it has more than just the act."

"So does porn sometimes." He pushed the blanket down and traced the perimeter of Oliver's left nipple with his fingertip.

"The clips I've seen online are guys walking into a room and then pretty much going at it."

"And in your fantasies it's not like that?" He moved to the other nipple and watched it pebble in response to his touch.

"Maybe eventually but—" Oliver rubbed his lips together and looked into Jaime's eyes. "You'll probably laugh, but oh well, you asked." He took a deep breath. "I have fantasies about everyday stuff. Like I'll be sitting on my couch playing *COD* and I'll think, 'If I had a boyfriend, we could be hanging out playing this together right now.' And then I'll think, 'Hey, I'm doing really well so he'd probably die first and then he'd be bored so he'd get on his knees and suck me off.'"

Jaime blinked a few times and then he chuckled. "That's great."

"Told you you'd laugh at me," Oliver said good-naturedly, and Jaime couldn't help noticing that the self-consciousness and shyness that had once crippled him were nowhere in sight.

"Not *at* you," Jaime assured him. "I'm laughing because your fantasies sound like mine."

"You daydream about getting blow jobs while you're playing *Call of Duty*?"

"Okay, maybe they're not *exactly* like mine, but the concept's the same."

"Yeah?"

"Mmm-hmm." Jaime lowered his hand to Oliver's groin and combed his fingers through his pubic bush.

"Tell me one."

"Let's see." Jaime let his mind wander away from that moment and to the evenings he spent alone. "Cooking doesn't make sense because I live alone so I end up meeting friends or work people for dinner a lot, but sometimes I'm too tired to be social and I get takeout or delivery. I'll be standing at my counter, biting into a mediocre turkey sandwich and I'll think about what it'd be like if I had a husband to come home to. Maybe he finished work early that day and the smell of a homemade dinner will greet me when I walk in the door or maybe he had a rough day too, and we'll putter around the kitchen together, getting a meal ready while we commiserate about whatever nonsense so-and-so did at the office. After dinner, we'll cuddle on the couch, and by the time we go to bed, we'll have forgotten about whatever was stressing us out and we'll make love until we're too tired to keep our eyes open." Lost in the mental images, it took Jaime several seconds to come back to the present. He curled his fingers under Oliver's balls and rubbed his thumb over the sensitive orbs. "See? I'm the boring middle-aged type."

"That's not boring," Oliver said breathlessly.

"No?" Jaime had hoped he and Oliver wanted the same things out of a relationship, but their escort-client dynamic hadn't given him much room to probe.

"No." Oliver swallowed hard and looked at him with yearning. "It's beautiful."

Up until that point, Jaime'd had to satisfy himself with getting to know as much as he could about Oliver without probing into his day-to-day life. Being privy to someone's deepest insecurities and most fervent desires while at the same time having to steer clear of what would normally be mundane topics frustrated him. Taking a chance that he could finally eliminate that barrier, Jaime said, "How are things at work? Anything interesting going on? Anything stressful?"

"Work's good." Oliver scrunched his eyebrows together. "There is one thing that's been frustrating."

"Tell me about it." Jaime moved his hand from Oliver's balls to his no longer flaccid dick.

"I'm working on an action game. Not just me, there's a team of us."

Jaime smiled, not at all surprised to learn he had even more in common with Oliver. "Programmer?"

"Designer. It's pretty much my dream job and it's been going really well and then, a couple of weeks ago, I had this conversation with a woman at work, and she pointed out that the female characters in our games look really... I can't remember the words she used but basically she was saying the women don't look right."

"Don't look right?"

"Yeah. You play RPG?"

Not as much as he used to, but he probably still knew more about Role Playing Games than most game designers, so he nodded.

"Okay. So you know how the players can choose some of the clothes? For the guys, it's like standard military uniforms or all black, maybe a chest plate, right? But whatever they pick, they're completely dressed in something that makes sense for the battle."

"Right."

"Have you ever noticed that the clothes for the women aren't like that?"

Jaime furrowed his brow as he thought about the women in RPG games. He hadn't been involved to that level of detail in years, and he was having trouble remembering games with female characters. "No, I haven't. What do they wear?"

"Things that wouldn't pass the dress code in my old high school, forget about making sense when they're sneaking through minefields or the jungle or an abandoned spacecraft. All the exposed skin would get torn up and they'd have really limited range of motion with their legs because their skirts or pants are so short and tight. And their chests are like—" Oliver shook his head. "The struggle is totally real. I was talking about it with Tamra, my friend at work, and we ran a simulation. Their waists would literally collapse under the weight of their boobs the way we design them. It's stupid."

"Sounds like it," Jaime agreed. "So are you doing it differently in the one you're working on now?"

"I'm trying, but you wouldn't believe how hard it is. After I talked with Tamra, I explained all this to the design team. They looked at me like I was stupid and said nobody would be interested in that player if she was ugly. So I told them it's not a matter of ugly, it's a matter of making sense. Like I pointed out that on a long mission, nobody would have time to cake on a bunch of makeup and use hairspray."

"What'd they say?"

"There are five of us and only one other guy agreed with me, but he's a little older and has kids, so the rest of the team told him he was pussy-whipped and blew us off. I can't even with these guys. I mean, I won't give up but seriously…"

Jaime was thankful the people he worked with had more sense. He wasn't connected to the day-to-day operations any longer, but he knew the executive team, and more importantly, he knew Jack. They'd never abide that type of mindset. "Sounds like you need to find a better company. Maybe one operating in the twenty-first century."

"Snow Storm is amazing. In the gaming world, it's considered like the top independent game producer."

Words stuck in Jaime's throat, and he stared at Oliver as he continued speaking.

"Plus, Tamra told me she's seen the same thing everywhere

she's worked. She says the problem is… I'm trying to think of her exact words. '*Systemic to the industry.*'" He sighed and shook his head. "I promised my niece we could test out the game I'm working on once we have it in Beta, and my sister's so proud of me for getting this job that she's willing to overlook the"—he raised his hands and scrunched his fingers in air quotes—"excessive violence, but I don't feel right about giving a thirteen-year-old a game where the only girl looks like some sort of sex doll, so I'll keep working to get the team on board with making the woman look normal. Anyway, that's my work drama. The whole thing is seriously dumb."

"You work at Snow Storm?" Jaime asked hoarsely.

"Yeah." Oliver dipped his chin bashfully. "When I got the job, I kept waiting for an email saying it was offered to the wrong person, but…" He shrugged. "I got lucky."

"I'm sure it has nothing to do with luck and everything to do with talent," Jaime said, needing to make clear that his reaction to the unexpected information didn't stem from any doubts about Oliver's skills. He took a deep breath and tried to slow his racing mind. This wasn't that big a deal. At least *he* didn't think it was a big deal. He'd just add it to the pile of lies by omission he eventually needed to explain to Oliver and find a way to make sure Oliver didn't think it was a big deal. No problem.

"Mostly I fell into the job," Oliver said, his tone a mix of excited and embarrassed, as if he was worried about bragging but too proud to stop himself from talking about his career. "When I lived in Oklahoma, I had a lot of free time and no social life so I messed around and designed a strategy game. I didn't think anyone would play it or anything, but I had nothing else to do so I figured why not." He raised one shoulder. "It wasn't horrible, so I uploaded it to itch.io. Next thing I knew, someone from

Snow Storm got in touch with me. They paid me a bunch of money for the game, and a little while after that, they offered me a job." His face lit up. "If I think about it too much, I start worrying I'm having a dream that I'll wake up from any second."

Choosing his words carefully, Jaime said, "I'm glad you have a job you enjoy, and I'm *really* glad the job is in Seattle."

"Me too." Oliver licked his bottom lip and pulled it between his teeth. "Jaime?"

"Yes?"

"Do you, uh, have plans for that?" Oliver looked down.

Following his gaze to the lump in the blanket, Jaime noticed he was still fondling what was now a nicely erect dick. Although his mind had been distracted by their conversation, his hand had apparently stayed on task.

"I sure do." He tightened his grip and grinned. "Fun plans."

Oliver's mouth dropped open in a quiet gasp.

"You've told me before that nothing's off the table so I assume that includes topping me?"

"Yes. I mean, no. I mean…" Oliver frowned. "I'm not in a mental place where I can figure out that sentence but topping is on the table. Bottoming is too."

Utterly charmed by that honest eagerness, Jaime leaned closer and brushed his lips over Oliver's, the movement pushing the blanket farther down. "Do you have any preferences on positions?"

Gripping the blanket, Oliver shook his head and said, "No. I'm good with whatever you want."

"I like sex and I like you, so combining the two is a sure bet as far as I'm concerned, but if you really want to know what turns me on…" He arched his eyebrows in question.

"Yeah." Oliver bobbed his head eagerly. "Tell me what that

is."

"Visual stimulation does it for me."

Oliver looked at him blankly.

"I want to watch you," Jaime whispered as he reached for Oliver's hands, still clenched around the blanket. Since the moment Jaime walked into the room, Oliver had been lying on his back and he hadn't moved from that position. Jaime hadn't gotten as far as he had in life and business without knowing how to read people, and Oliver, in particular, was an open book. The man was self-conscious about his appearance, and he thought his weight was less noticeable at that angle. "I want to see every inch of your body while you're moving and pushing inside me." Slowly, Jaime tugged the blanket away, exposing more skin. "I *like* your body." He had said the same thing an hour earlier but understood that he was working against a belief that had been ingrained over a lifetime so he'd need to repeat that particular truth more than a few times before it sunk in.

Sitting up, Jaime pulled the blanket away and let his eyes roam over the man who was now completely exposed to him. "I love that you don't shave." He slid his fingers through the hair on Oliver's chest and stomach. "So sexy." As he lowered his hand to Oliver's groin, he dipped his face down and licked his cockhead. "Mmm." One hand gripping the base of Oliver's shaft and the other cupping his balls, Jaime swiped his tongue against the rounded edges of his glans.

"Jaime." Oliver's thighs shook and his fingers dug into the mattress.

"You're not small." He dropped his mouth over Oliver's dick and sucked his way up.

"Oh God." Oliver stared at him wide-eyed.

"And I haven't done this in a long time." Jaime wasn't one

for sleeping around, never had been. "So we'll need to start with fingers." He leaned across Oliver to the nightstand, pulled the drawer open, and retrieved the lube and condoms he had stashed there earlier. "The question is"—back in his spot beside Oliver, he folded his legs underneath his butt—"who's going to do it? Me or you?"

Mouth open and breath labored, Oliver made a strangled sound but didn't manage words.

"That's very flattering." Jaime clicked the cap on the bottle, drizzled slick onto his fingers, and pressed the bottle closed. "How about I start?" He rose to his knees, reached between his legs, and circled his fingertip over his pucker. "You can join in any time." Slowly, Jaime slipped his finger into his ass, his eyes closing reflexively. The feeling wasn't bad but it didn't turn him on either. He carefully slicked his inner walls and wriggled his finger from side to side, reminding his muscles how to stretch and accommodate the wanted invasion.

"Jaime?"

"Yes?" Jaime opened his eyes to see Oliver sitting up, staring at him.

"Will you—" He took a deep breath as if gathering his nerves. "I want to see you touching yourself. Can you show me?" He licked his lips. "Like you, uh, did in the living room earlier?"

Jaime's ass clenched at the memory of Oliver's mouth working him over. "Happy to." He lowered himself to his back, tucked his knees up and out, and used one hand to hold them. Then, with his attention focused on Oliver's face, he slid his middle finger into his hole.

"Oh," Oliver gasped. "That's…" He shook his head.

"It's what?" Jaime asked, his voice strained. Fingers in his ass had never done it for him, but Oliver's expression definitely did.

"So hot." Oliver reached a shaking hand forward and gently skimmed the puckered skin surrounding Jaime's buried finger. "I can't believe I get to touch you like this."

"You can touch me however you want." Jaime slid his finger out, wrapped his hand around Oliver's and led him to his hole. "Go ahead."

Oliver's breath stuttered and he swallowed hard, but then he nodded and sank his finger into Jaime. "It's soft." He pushed deeper. "And warm." Gaze flickering from Jaime's ass to his chest, Oliver said, "Did you know that your nipples get darker when you're turned on?"

"They do?"

"Uh-huh." Oliver focused on Jaime's chest. "I noticed it last time, and it's happening now too."

The conversation made Jaime take stock of his nipples. "They tingle."

"You said they're sensitive?"

"Very," Jaime said breathlessly.

"What if I…" Finger still working Jaime's hole, Oliver rose to his knees, planted his free hand next to Jaime's side, and lowered his mouth to Jaime's chest. "All week, I've been thinking about the way your skin tastes." He swiped his tongue over Jaime's hardened nipple. "So good." A few more rounds with his tongue and then Oliver took him into his mouth and suckled.

"Ungh," Jaime moaned, hands instinctively moving to the back of Oliver's head and holding him in place. "Like that. Suck them like that."

With his finger continuing to prod Jaime's hole, Oliver went from one nipple to the other, working them with lips, tongue, and teeth until they were sore little pleasure centers protruding from Jaime's chest.

"Damn, Oliver." Jaime arched his back, trying to get closer. "Time to glove up, okay?" When Oliver didn't move, Jaime patted the mattress blindly until the condom wrapper crinkled under his fingertips. A few moments of fiddling and he had it open. "Sit back a second." He tightened his stomach muscles and pushed himself up to a sitting position, knocking Oliver off his chest in the process.

Lips swollen and eyes heavy-lidded, Oliver looked at him in confusion.

"I'm so hard," he said by way of explanation as he took the condom out of the wrapper. "And I really need you to fuck me before I come." He slid it down Oliver's cock, found the lube, and slicked him up. "You're beautiful, you know that?"

"You make me feel like that could be true," Oliver said quietly.

Jaime curled his hand around Oliver's nape and brushed their lips together. "It *is* true." He tilted his head to the side and licked his way into Oliver's mouth as he stroked his dick.

"I want you," Oliver said, voice breaking.

"Take me." Jaime lowered himself to his back and curled his hips up, putting his ass on display. "Show me what that big, sexy body can do."

Still on his knees, Oliver shuffled forward, gripped his cock, and pressed it to Jaime's hole. Lips parted and chest heaving, Oliver continued forward, stretching Jaime with welcome pressure.

"This feels amazing," Oliver said. When his groin finally nestled against Jaime's cheeks and his cock was completely buried, Oliver reached for Jaime's leg, pulled it against his chest, and kissed Jaime's calf. "*You* feel amazing."

"So do you." Jaime curled his free leg around the back of

Oliver's hip and set his ankle on the top of Oliver's butt.

Oliver pulled out and then drove back in again, more rapidly this time. He found his rhythm quickly, clutching Jaime's leg as he thrust in and out of his body. Skin slapped against skin and both men moaned.

When Oliver's fingers started twitching against his calf and his eyes took on a wild, desperate look, Jaime knew he was close. Eyes roaming over the thick, hairy, sweat-slick body above him, Jaime's breath caught. This was his ideal image of masculinity.

"Oliver," he moaned, reaching for his own dick. "Yes." He took himself in hand and stroked furiously, ready to fall over the edge.

The sight of Jaime beating off was apparently too much for Oliver to take because he cried out, ground his hips into Jaime, and came with a shout.

"Don't stop." Jaime thrust his hips, encouraging Oliver to move. "Just need a little more."

After blinking a few times, Oliver drew in a deep breath and began pumping again. His dick hadn't fully softened yet so Jaime continued enjoying the stretch in his hole and the drag of Oliver's cockhead against his gland while he worked his own cock faster. Then Oliver caressed Jaime's stomach and chest and, with his gaze glued to Jaime's, traced Jaime's areolas with this thumbs before squeezing them between his thumb and finger and twisting.

"Oliver!" Jaime shouted, the wave of pleasure hitting him hard and fast. "Ungh." His back arched and hot seed flowed over his fingers and across his stomach. "Yes!"

Chest still heaving, Oliver stared at him in awe. "Wow."

"Wow is right." Limbs suddenly twenty pounds heavier, Jaime lowered his arms to his sides and flopped his legs on the mattress. "I'm too tired to make it to the bathroom." He reached for the tissue box on the nightstand and did a mediocre job wiping himself off. "I know I should probably take a shower but my legs don't work anymore."

Oliver's face lit up. "Since I'm responsible for your condition, I'll get something to clean you up." He scooted back slowly, removing his dick from Jaime's now sensitive hole, and then leaned down and pressed his face to Jaime's neck. "And I'm glad you're not showering." He licked a swath down Jaime's neck and over to his armpit. "I dream about your scent, now I get to actually have it all night." One more lick and then Oliver climbed out of bed and walked into the attached bathroom.

Jaime sighed contentedly. He had nearly given up his hope of being with a man who aroused him physically, who he enjoyed spending time with socially, and who intrigued him intellectually. Then he happened to be in the right place at the right time and he met Oliver Barnaby, who pushed all his buttons without trying. Luck had definitely been on Jaime's side that night. Now it was up to him to prove he could be the man Oliver had been hoping to find.

Chapter 9

THE SOUND OF a door opening registered in Jaime's mind at the exact same moment Rex jumped off his lap and barked his way to the mudroom. Kiki and Lulu looked up but didn't leave their perch in one of Rex's many dog beds.

"Don't overexert yourselves," Jaime joked as he picked up the remote and clicked the television off. "I'm sure Rex will be able to take care of the big bad robber all by himself."

"Gone less than forty-eight hours and I'm a robber in my own home."

"Hey." Jaime stood and turned toward the cased opening to the cozy family room. He hoped Jack wasn't planning to hire a designer to remodel that room in the same style as the world's most uncomfortable living room. "I was just teasing my girls."

"Don't get up." Jack waved his hand in Jaime's direction. "I'll come sit with you." He walked toward the sofa, Rex at his heels.

"Go ahead and relax. I'll get you a drink and then you can tell me how it went." He walked toward the bar in the corner of the room. "Was it a 'bottle of water' kind of trip or a 'liquor in the afternoon' kind of trip?"

"Scotch," Jack said tiredly. "Bring the whole bottle."

Jaime winced. "She's getting worse?"

"Yes, she is." Jack sighed and fell into a well-worn leather armchair. The dog immediately jumped onto his lap. Jack buried his fingers in Rex's fur and petted him. "How did Rex do?"

"He missed you." Jaime poured some Chivas Regal into a whiskey glass. "But he was perfect as usual." He tucked a water bottle under each arm and picked up the glass in one hand and the Chivas in the other. "When are you going back?"

"Not sure." Jack rubbed his palm over the back of his neck. "Carol and Rob are there this week. We'll see how my mom's doing when it's time for them to go home."

"How is Carol?" Jaime handed Jack the glass and then set the Chivas and the water bottle on the end table beside him.

"Fine." Jaime picked up the scotch and brought it to his nose. "At least I think she's fine." He swirled the drink and sniffed it. "We didn't get to talk much. When I wasn't meeting with my mom's doctors, I was in the room with her and the last thing she needs is stress."

"Hearing about Carol's life constitutes stress?" Jaime unscrewed his water bottle. "I take it that means your mother still can't stand Rob?"

"What do you think?" Jack sipped his drink slowly.

The first time Jack's sister had brought her then boyfriend home to meet her family, Rob had sat on his butt while everyone else helped clear the table, and when they had been watching the game, he had handed Carol his empty bottle or glass every time he wanted a refill. He had also alternated between avoiding any contact with Jaime and Jack and trying to one-up them. It was an awkward mix of gay-cootie fear and I'm-more-of-a-man-than-you ego.

"I think a leopard rarely changes his spots." Jaime sat on the couch.

"Agreed." Jack swallowed more amber liquid. "He shakes my hand without cringing or trying to break it now, so I guess that's an improvement."

"Yay," Jaime said sarcastically. "The big question is if he's decent to your sister." He laid his head on the rounded sofa arm, stretched his body across the four overfilled cushions, and propped his ankles on the other arm.

"I don't know." Jack shook his head. "Carol chooses to stay married to him. That has to mean something, right?"

"Hopefully it means she loves him." Jaime raised his right arm above his head and tugged it with his left hand, stretching out his muscles. "Doesn't mean he isn't a dick."

"Nope, it doesn't." Jack sighed and tipped his glass against his lips.

They sat in comfortable silence, the hum of the air conditioning and the occasional snuffs from the dogs the only sounds in the room. As much as he hated ending the peaceful moment and adding stress to Jack's already rough few days, they needed to talk about Oliver.

"The guy I was telling you about?" Jaime said, his gaze fixed on the ceiling.

"Yeah?" Jack's voice was neutral. Too neutral to be natural.

"He stayed over here with me Friday and Saturday night. Left this morning."

"So things are going well?"

Jaime nodded.

"I'm happy for you." Even though Jack sounded strained, Jaime knew the sentiment was sincere.

"He works at Snow Storm."

Jack's legs had been stretched out in front of him, but in reaction to that revelation, he jerked to a sitting position. "What?"

"I didn't know until this weekend."

"You've been seeing this guy long enough to be serious and you didn't know where he worked?" Jack said disbelievingly.

Jaime didn't doubt Jack's trust in him, that was a given, but the situation was unusual. "This thing's had a..." Jaime tried to think of the right words to say enough but not too much. "Unique kind of start."

"That means I know him," Jack mumbled, more to himself than to Jaime.

"I doubt it." Jaime turned his head to the side so he could see Jack's face. "He's a designer. Entry level from the sound of it. Company's too big for you to know every person."

"Two hundred people isn't that big. I know everyone who works for me."

Jaime arched his eyebrows.

"Eventually," Jack grudgingly added. "I know them all eventually."

"Oliver's new. Been there around three months. Maybe a little less."

Lips pinched, Jack furrowed his brow in thought. "Oliver Barnaby?"

Jaime nodded.

"I used to come by and introduce myself to new employees during their first few weeks, but we've been slammed with one crisis after another and my mom's been sick and redecorating the house took more of my time than I anticipated so—" Jack let out a deep breath. "I didn't realize I was letting work slide."

He had planned to talk to Jack about the issues with Snow Storm's female characters, but the exhaustion mapped across Jack's face made Jaime realize work could wait.

"Hey," he said softly. When Jack met his gaze, he continued speaking. "You don't owe me any excuses about how you run the company."

"It's half yours, so technically—"

"Technically, you don't owe me any excuses about how you run the company," Jaime repeated. "That aside, everyone I meet with confirms what I already know: you're doing a great job."

The two of them had founded Snow Storm when they were a couple. When they ended that relationship eight years earlier, Jaime had turned his attention to dealing with outside entities and stepped away from the day-to-day operations of the business, leaving it in Jack's hands. Jaime's focus had resulted in an exponential increase in their distribution channels, more efficient manufacturing methods, an improved marketing and promotion process, and a seemingly endless string of buy-out offers. The last one was in large part due to Jack's skill and effort running the company.

"I remember approving his hire. Lucas Holster came across his designs. Said he's got raw talent."

"I don't have first-hand knowledge of Oliver's skill, but he's smart and dedicated so I'm sure Lucas is right."

"Well, he's your boyfriend now, right? That means I have two reasons to meet him." Jack cleared his throat and spoke in a formal tone. "Hi. My name is Jack Storm and I'm the CEO of Snow Storm. On behalf of the entire team, we're glad to have you on board. Also, if you're being sexually harassed by a high-level executive, like say, an owner, make sure to let me know. I'll personally drive you to the EEOC office and lend you a pen to fill out a complaint."

"Lovely. Thanks for the loyalty."

Jack laughed.

Rolling his eyes, Jaime finished his water, wiped the back of his hand across his mouth, and said, "Give me another week or two to get that boyfriend thing locked up. Then you can take on the role of Master Chief."

DRUMMING HIS FINGERTIPS against the back of his phone, Jaime looked out through the floor to ceiling windows in his home office and enjoyed the serenity of Lake Washington as he considered his next move with Oliver. Without planning or discussion, he and Oliver had fallen into a comfortable pattern of seeing each other on Friday nights. He now knew Oliver well enough to realize the introverted man preferred predictability over spontaneity, something Jaime found utterly charming. But if he wanted a chance at building a future with Oliver, a real, honest future, then he had to transition their interactions from hidden liaisons weighed down by the pretense of a financial exchange to normal dates. And he needed to do it quickly. It was only a matter of time before Oliver stopped being too nervous to see what was right in front of him, and then the ever-growing tower of misconceptions would topple and possibly destroy their budding relationship in its wake.

Step one had been the text exchanges he had instigated after the first time Oliver had contacted him to set up a meeting. Slowly, he'd started sending messages that had nothing to do with scheduling. A funny picture, an interesting anecdote, a follow-up question on something they'd discussed. In the beginning, Oliver had only responded, but it didn't take long before he also initiated contact, and now they texted each other throughout the day.

The next step had been their Friday night at the Madison Pub and their weekend at Jack's house. They had spent time together in public and surpassed their three-hour time clock.

Now Jaime needed to find a way for them to interact when sex was clearly off the table. Not that Jaime didn't enjoy the physical side of Oliver; he honestly couldn't think of a man he had lusted for as ferociously. But he had to decimate his introductory role as a sexual teacher who wanted nothing other than money in exchange for his time and services because, in truth, he wanted something very different from Oliver. In his quiet, hopeful moments, he dared to admit to himself that he wanted everything.

Wanting to start this new chapter in their relationship as he intended to continue, Jaime thought about how he would pursue a man who interested him. Simple and straightforward had always been his preferred approach in work and in his personal life. Things with Oliver had veered off the track from the beginning and Jaime had gone along with it because he could see how much Oliver had needed the crutches he had put in place. But now it was time to stop pretending and see if they could fit together as well in real life as they did in the semi-fantasy.

He rolled his phone over and tapped out a text. "*How's your day going?*"

Almost immediately, his phone dinged with Oliver's response. "*It's more starting than going right now. ;) Early morning for you?*"

A quick glance at the clock revealed it wasn't quite eight thirty. Though he was normally a night owl, thoughts about how to handle the situation with Oliver had made sleeping a challenge so he had given up and started his day a couple of hours ahead of his usual schedule. Taking Oliver's question as a lead-in, Jaime forged ahead with his plan: a bit of small talk and then a date. "*Very. I got extra work in so I'll be able to wrap up early. Can I take you to lunch?*"

This time there was a noticeable delay before Oliver responded. "*Sure. Where?*"

Not wanting to cut their time together short, Jaime chose a restaurant near Oliver. "*How about Bis on Main at 1?*"

A few seconds and then another ding. "*Sounds good.*"

At forty years old, Jaime was well acquainted with relationships, hookups, and dates, but transitioning from a sex worker to a boyfriend was brand new territory, so he carefully chose the words in his final text. "*Great. I'm looking forward to our date.*"

Oliver didn't respond, which could have meant he had gotten busy with work or that he didn't see anything left to say, but Jaime was fairly certain the actual reason was that Oliver was staring at his phone and contemplating every possible interpretation of the word "date."

"HI. I HAVE a reservation under Jaime at one o'clock. Table for two."

Glancing down at the book in front of her, the hostess nodded and said, "Your table will be ready in a few minutes."

"Thanks." Jaime stepped aside to make room for the group that came in after him.

It was ten minutes shy of one o'clock, but despite being early, Jaime was surprised hyper-punctual Oliver wasn't already waiting on him. One of the many things he admired about Oliver was his thoughtfulness. Although he struggled when it came to interacting with others, Oliver set aside his own nerves and arrived to places on the early side of on time. That type of consideration for people's feelings and needs was evident in the bedroom too, where all Oliver wanted was to please his partner. There wasn't an ounce of selfishness in Oliver, and despite being talented and bright, he wasn't arrogant or showy. The more Jaime got to know him, the higher his admiration and desire for Oliver grew. And the sexy outside wrapping appealed to him just as much as Oliver's intelligence and heart. For the first time in his life, Jaime believed he had found someone he wanted, inside and out.

His chest tight with longing, Jaime took a calming breath and reached for a distraction. Both he and Jack believed digital distribution was the future of their industry and the best way to save on overhead and keep their prices affordable, but if they wanted to remain competitive in the present, they had to get their games on retail shelves. He had been exchanging notes with a promising new brick and mortar distributor before he had left for lunch, so he pulled out his phone to check if he had made progress.

"I'll take you to your table now," said the hostess.

"Great." Jaime slid his phone into his pocket and followed her, his mind still on the email.

"Here you go." The hostess set two menus on a table tucked into a corner between a window and two walls. The view was nice, the privacy even better. "Your server will be right over to get your drink order."

"Thank you." Jaime sat down and reflexively picked up his menu.

"It *is* you. I saw you walking by, and I called your name, but you didn't answer, so I started doubting myself and thought it was wishful thinking but no. It's you!"

At the sound of the happy voice, Jaime glanced up.

"Kevin!" He pushed his chair back and stood to greet his old friend. "I didn't hear you." He leaned in for a hug and a wave of nostalgia washed over him from the familiarity of the act. "It's been too long."

Like he had with his neighborhood and his role at Snow Storm, Jaime had distanced himself from his friends when he and Jack separated. Ten years sharing a life with someone meant their social circles had been intertwined, and although the end of their relationship had been mutual in a technical sense, Jaime had never harbored any illusions about the cause. Taking away the future Jack had counted on was bad enough; Jaime refused to jeopardize his support system.

"And whose fault is that?" Hand on his hip, Kevin arched a perfectly shaped eyebrow.

"Mine." Jaime put his hand on Kevin's shoulder and squeezed it. "Doesn't mean I haven't missed you guys."

His expression softening, Kevin stepped closer. "You have a permanent spot at the table, Jaime. Eight days, eight months, or eight years won't change that. All the guys would love to have you back."

Jaime had never had trouble filling his time or making friends, but the men he and Jack had known since their first days in the city held a special place in his heart. They had been his family of choice, and losing them had hurt.

"You do know Jack would say the same thing if he were standing here, right?" Kevin whispered.

Swallowing thickly, Jaime dipped his chin. "I know." And for the first time, Jaime would actually believe Jack meant the words. Enough time had passed for them both to regain their footing in life and for the dynamics of their friendship to solidify. "It really has been too long."

"Come to my Halloween party. Saturday night. Eight thirty. Costumes optional but very much encouraged." When Jaime didn't immediately respond, Kevin cupped his cheek and met his gaze. "The whole crew's going to be there. Come to the party, Jaime."

Jaime took a deep breath and let it out. "Can I bring a date?"

"Dates are even more encouraged than costumes." Kevin beamed. "I'm getting out of here before you change your mind." He leaned up, kissed Jaime's cheek, and then turned around and waved over his shoulder. "I'll send you an email with the details. See you Saturday. Wear something slutty!"

As was no doubt his intention, Kevin's parting comment eased the weight of the nostalgic melancholy that had settled over Jaime. He chuckled softly as he pulled out his phone and texted Jack. "*I ran into Kevin. He invited me to his Halloween party.*"

"*Good. Bring your boyfriend.*"

Relieved, Jaime smiled. "*Working on it.*"

Chapter 10

"HI. I'M MEETING someone for lunch. I'm not sure if he's here yet. He's got brown hair and green eyes. He's about six three, well built—"

"Is his name Jaime?" the hostess asked, grinning.

Oliver's face heated at the realization of how he had sounded. Oh well, if she had seen Jaime, she had to understand. "Yeah, that's him."

"Right this way."

Tugging at his shirtsleeves, Oliver followed behind her and tried not to be nervous about why he was there. Jaime's text had said he was looking forward to their *date*, but that word could mean many different things, and Oliver didn't want to jump to any conclusions. Maybe Jaime needed to discuss something, not that Oliver had any clue what that could possibly be. He developed video games for a living; that wasn't a service most people found themselves needing.

"Miss! I need to speak with a manager." A customer stepped in front of the hostess, blocking their path.

"I'm showing this gentleman to his table and then—"

The customer shook his head. "I'm in a rush. I need to speak with the manager now."

The hostess looked flustered, so Oliver said, "If you point me in the direction of the table, I'm sure I won't have any trouble finding him."

"Thank you." She looked grateful. "He's right over there." She pointed to a three-quarter length wall.

"Got it." Oliver wound his way around the tables as quickly as he could, not wanting to be late, but the sight that greeted him on the other side of the wall stopped him in his tracks: Jaime and another man, leaning close together, touching, and whispering intimately.

Right away, he realized he was seeing Jaime with another client, and he instinctively stepped back behind the wall, needing space between himself and the unwelcome vision. He had known why Jaime was with him from the first moment they'd met but as the weeks passed and they spent more and more time together, he had begun to believe they weren't just an escort and a client. He had naïvely thought the way Jaime touched him, looked at him, and spoke to him made him different from other people, special. But a front-row view of Jaime with another man showed Oliver that what he had considered unique was simply Jaime being good at his job.

He leaned against the wall and wiped his clammy hands on his pants while he waited for his lungs to stop working overtime. Instead of sticking to his plan of bettering himself so he could meet people and hopefully get a boyfriend, Oliver had blown all his extra money and stupidly developed feelings for someone who saw him as a paycheck. Bits and pieces of Jaime's conversation drifted over, stabbing at Oliver's racing heart until, finally, the man with Jaime scheduled his next appointment and left.

A large part of Oliver wanted to follow him, not to confront him or even to speak to him, but to walk out of the restaurant and get away from the pain and disappointment. But he had promised to meet Jaime for lunch and standing him up would be rude. After all, Oliver had no right to be surprised, let alone upset, that Jaime had other clients. He gave himself another couple of minutes to calm down and then he squared his shoulders and approached the table.

"There you are." Jaime smiled, rose from his seat, and held his arm out. "Did work get busy?"

If Oliver answered that question truthfully, he would have to explain why he was late, something he wanted to avoid. But neither did he want to lie, so he went with redirection instead. "How was your morning?" he asked, ignoring Jaime's out-stretched arm in favor of pulling out the empty chair and sitting down. It was the first time he hadn't wanted to touch Jaime and the feeling struck him as wrong. "Did you get a lot of"—he swallowed the sudden thickness in his throat—"work done?"

"Decent amount."

Jaime's tone sounded weird but Oliver couldn't bring himself to look him in the face.

"That's good." He picked up the menu and stared at it blindly. The words were fuzzy but it gave him an excuse to avert his gaze.

After an uncomfortably long silence, Jaime said, "Listen to this crazy story. Yesterday afternoon I was at a meeting and a woman walked in who I hadn't seen in nearly a year. We were making small talk and catching up when she asked me if I believed in feng shui." Jaime paused, and from his peripheral vision, Oliver saw that he was watching him. He didn't look away from the menu. "Do you know what that is?"

"Nuh-uh." Oliver shook his head.

"From what I understand it's a Chinese philosophy where you're supposed to design things a certain way to have good energy. Well, anyway, two years ago, this woman and her husband bought a new house, and as soon as they moved in, they were hit with a streak of bad luck. Her husband lost his job, her son started having trouble in school, her old house wasn't selling even though they reduced the price below everything else in the neighborhood, the pipes on her new house clogged and flooded everything, she couldn't get pregnant, her car kept breaking down. Basically, everything that could go wrong did. She was stressed, her husband was stressed, her kid was struggling, and it got to the point where she thought they'd have to walk away from both houses because they couldn't keep covering the mortgages."

Despite himself, Oliver set the menu aside and looked at Jaime. "That's terrible."

"I know. But here's where it gets good. One day she came home from work and her husband told her he had been looking on *Backpage* for jobs and he came across an ad for a feng shui expert. He paid the guy a thousand dollars to come to the house and give them advice on how to harmonize. She flipped out because they didn't have money to spare but there was nothing she could do about it at that point so she didn't stop her husband from following the steps in the guy's plan. According to her, it wasn't much. Moving some furniture around. Putting potted flowers on the porch. Planting a few things in certain places. Painting the front door. Simple, cheap stuff.

"They did all of it over the weekend and then, on Monday, her husband got an email from a company who saw his resume online. A few rounds of interviews later, he got hired and now he makes twice what he did at his previous job. Her son's school said they'd done testing and his scores were off the charts. Apparently, the kid is some kind of genius and he was having trouble in class because he was bored, so they transferred him to a special program and he's thriving. They won the grand prize in a raffle they'd entered outside the grocery store and got a new car. Her old house sold at their asking price. The home insurance company paid for their floors to be fixed from the flood and they replaced all their furniture. And then the reason she had been out of the office—after a year of trying, she finally got pregnant with twins. She had to be on bedrest during the end of the pregnancy but they have two healthy girls."

"Wow."

"I know." Jaime smiled. "It's a crazy story with a good moral."

"Hire a feng shui expert?"

"*Backpage* is a good place to find a happy ending even if it doesn't happen exactly the way you expected."

Thirty minutes earlier, Oliver would have agreed with that sentiment. After all, Jaime had come into his life from a *Backpage* ad. But now he knew there was no happy ending in his future, at least not one with Jaime. He picked up his menu again, needing a way to hide.

"Are you okay?" Jaime asked, his voice soft and concerned.

"Yeah."

Jaime put his hand on the top of the menu and pushed it down. A smile no longer graced his face. "Then why won't you look at me?"

The waiter's arrival saved Oliver from answering.

"I'm sorry to keep you waiting. Are you ready to order?"

After a long pause, Jaime sighed and said, "I'll have the seared cod," not moving his gaze from Oliver.

"Excellent choice. And for you, sir?"

Despite having had the menu in front of his face for nearly ten minutes, Oliver had no idea what the restaurant offered. "I, uh…" He picked the menu up and scrambled to figure out what to get.

"Do you want me to order for you?" Jaime offered.

"Sure," Oliver said, relieved.

Jaime shifted his gaze to the waiter. "He'll have the steak frites and we'll both start with the house salad, please."

"I'll get more water for you. Do you want anything else to drink?" the waiter asked as he took the menus. "Wine?"

"I'll have an iced tea." Jaime looked at him. "Oliver?"

"Water's good."

With a nod and a smile, the waiter walked away and took with him the only viable way to avoid the unwelcome tension between them.

"What's wrong?" Jaime asked.

He was Jaime's client, not his boyfriend, so Oliver knew he had no right to be upset. But knowledge didn't stop the sick feeling that had taken root in his stomach, and he couldn't seem to stop himself from treating Jaime badly for something that wasn't his fault.

"I'm sorry," he rasped.

"What are you sorry about?" Jaime leaned across the table and looked at him beseechingly. "Talk to me, baby."

The word squeezed Oliver's heart as if it were a touch. "You called me baby."

Jaime nodded.

Searching his eyes, Oliver whispered, "What does that mean?" When Jaime scrunched his eyebrows together in confusion, Oliver licked his lips and tried another approach. "When you texted me this morning, you said this was a date, but it's not, right? I'm your client so this is what? A business meeting?"

For a few seconds Jaime remained silent, his expression contemplative. Then he said, "I suppose that depends on what you want this to be. When we met, you said your goal was to have a relationship. Do you still want that? And, more specifically, do you want it with me?"

Oliver's heart screamed "yes" in response to that question. He had already fallen for Jaime, even if he hadn't wanted to admit that to himself. But before he replied, he had to decide if he could handle having a relationship with someone who had sex with other people, let alone someone who did it for money. If Jaime were his boyfriend, Oliver would eventually have to introduce him to his family and friends. How would he explain Jaime's work to them? Treating a theoretical escort with respect despite his job had made Oliver feel enlightened and open-minded, but now that he had feelings for Jaime, deep feelings, he wasn't at all open to Jaime being intimate with other people.

"I asked you on a date because that's what I want," Jaime said. "But dating won't work if the only way you won't be nervous around me is when I'm a guy you pay."

"The money has nothing to do with how I feel when I'm with you," Oliver said firmly.

Jaime arched his eyebrows and tilted his head to the side.

"It did at the beginning," Oliver admitted. "But now that I know you—" He bit his lip. Jaime made him feel desirable, interesting, wanted, and safe. "You don't make me nervous." At least not for the reasons Jaime meant. Oliver doubted he'd be able to get over Jaime as easily as he had his ex-boyfriend so his anxiety now stemmed from a worry that he was in over his head with a man who had no real interest in him.

"Not nervous is good." Jaime's eyes softened and his lips turned up at the corners. "Does that mean you're ready to spend time with me with no money involved?"

If he said yes, he would have to figure out how to deal with knowing his boyfriend was sleeping with other men. But if he said no, Jaime wouldn't be his boyfriend. Oliver wasn't sure how he would handle the former, but the latter was completely unacceptable.

"Yes." Oliver nodded. "I want to be with you, so if you want to be with me too, then—" He took a deep breath. "Yes, I'm ready for that."

"BECAUSE I DON'T like sports," Tamra said, sounding irritated.

"You don't have to like softball. We just need three girls on the team."

Swallowing down his laughter, Oliver turned his chair to the right. Chad was standing next to Tamra's desk, his back to Oliver. From his angle, he could make eye contact with Tamra, so he grinned at her. She rolled her eyes.

"I understand that, Chad, but I don't want to spend my free time doing something I don't enjoy."

"Figures you wouldn't get it," Chad said, sounding disgusted.

Not acknowledging him, she turned to her computer.

Apparently that wasn't how he had expected her to respond to his insult because he continued hovering by her desk. "It's a company team."

"This isn't part of our job duties. It's just something you decided to put together." She started typing.

"I don't make the rules," he said, either misunderstanding her or choosing to ignore her. "The league does."

"Find a different league."

"All the corporate leagues make you have at least three girls."

"Find other *women* to play."

"Linda Fisch said she'd do it but I need three girls and you know there aren't many working here."

"I know." She continued typing.

"Why can't you be a team player? It's just softball!"

Rising to his feet, Oliver said, "Hey, Tamra."

"Yes?"

"We're going to be late to that meeting." He walked over to her.

She blinked a few times and then understanding crossed over her face. "That's right." She pulled her purse from her bottom drawer and pushed her chair back. "I lost track of time." She walked around the desk, said, "See you later, Chad," and approached Oliver.

"Starbucks?" Oliver said under his breath.

"Works for me."

They stayed quiet until they stepped into the elevator and then Tamra said, "Do you think he believes we have a meeting at five thirty?"

"Do you care what he believes?" Oliver said, frustrated with the way Chad had been speaking to his friend.

"Not really, but if he doesn't buy the meeting thing, he'll think we're doing something else, and knowing Chad, that something else will be of the naked variety."

Eyes wide, Oliver turned his head to look at her and said, "Really?"

She shrugged. "Probably. Do you know him?"

"No."

"He's one of those guys who always talks about his conquests, but if I were placing bets, I'd peg him for a virgin."

Oliver started coughing.

"What?"

"Nothing," he rasped and then cleared his throat.

"Please don't tell me you have the hots for that asshole?"

"No!" Oliver furiously shook his head. "Absolutely not." He also wouldn't tell her that he was as uncomfortable as a teenager when it came to talking about sex or that a couple of months earlier he hadn't been all that far from being a virgin himself.

"Good." She sighed. "He tries to get that dumb softball league going every year, and every year, he doesn't have enough people, yet somehow this is *my* fault."

"Snow Storm really does need to hire more women."

"They do, but it's tough in tech, you know? There aren't a lot of us." The elevator doors opened and they walked out. "Besides, he can't ever find enough men to fill the team either."

"We're all too busy playing VR."

She snorted. "Totally. If this was virtual softball, we could field two teams no problem."

"Especially if Chad wasn't on them," he joked, playfully bumping his side against her.

"Oh my God. For real. That guy is such a schmuck. If he isn't harassing people about softball or telling anyone who'll listen about how he got lucky over the weekend, he'll be extolling the virtues of his raw, gluten-free, vegan diet."

"He's vegan and gluten-free?" Oliver asked, frowning as he tried to think of what a person with those combined restrictions could eat, especially if they couldn't cook their food.

"Allegedly." Tamra pulled open the Starbucks door, and Oliver held onto it and waited for her to step inside. "Which makes me wonder how he has the energy to compete in all the triathlons he's always going on and on about."

"That reminds me, I do know him!" Oliver said excitedly.

"On my first or second day, I got to a meeting early, and he was in the conference room, talking about his vacation. Something about swimming Alcatraz."

"Yep. That's Chad," Tamra said, looking at him and rolling her eyes. The person in line ahead of them completed her order and left. "We're all just waiting for the day he starts bragging about his dick size."

The barista laughed, which got Oliver's attention. He looked at the man and noticed the way he was staring at Tamra.

"We're up," Oliver said to Tamra and then he stepped to the side so she could get closer to the counter. And the barista.

"Hi. I'll have a grande cinnamon dolce latte, a venti iced coffee with milk and two pumps of sweetener, and a chocolate croissant."

Hearing her place his order along with hers, Oliver pulled out his wallet.

"It's my treat," Tamra said, waving him off. "Consider it a thank-you for coming up with a plan to get me away from Chad before I said something he'd regret."

"You don't have to—"

"Don't argue with me," she said, giving Oliver a pointed look as she handed her credit card to the barista. "I've had my fill of male ego today."

The barista laughed again, his eyes still glued to Tamra.

"Thank you." Oliver dropped his wallet back into this pocket.

"No problem," Tamra said, taking her receipt and walking toward the tables.

Oliver picked up his croissant, rushed after her, and quietly said, "He was looking at you."

"Who?" Tamra sat down.

"The barista." Oliver furtively glanced toward the counter.

"People tend to do that when they're taking your order and ringing you up." She reached across the table and tore off a piece of Oliver's croissant. "I should have gotten a muffin."

"Why didn't you?"

"I don't know." She scratched her forehead. "Thought I'd try a diet."

"You're not fat." Tamra tended to wear loose clothing and layers, but from Oliver's perspective, she was curvy but slender.

"You're gay. You don't understand."

"Oh really?" he said sarcastically. "You're going to tell me that as a gay man I have no understanding of male body type expectations?"

Her cheeks reddened. "Never mind. That was a dumb thing to say. I guess anyone who sleeps with men has this stupid pressure. The struggle is totally real." She sighed. "Am I allowed to say men suck or is that sexist?"

"You can say it." Oliver smirked. "And I can tell you that I really like guys who suck."

After a second, Tamra threw her head back and laughed. "Nicely played!"

"Here are your drinks." They both looked up at the barista who was placing cups on their table. Normally their names were called when their order was ready at the counter. "I, uh, know you usually get the chocolate chip muffin so I brought you one," said the barista as he set a muffin in front of Tamra. He fiddled with the gauge in his ear, mumbled, "It's on me," and then rushed away.

"Say thank you," Oliver hissed.

Tamra blinked furiously, her jaw hanging open, and then she shook her head as if to clear it and yelled after him, "Thanks for the muffin! I like your hair."

"I like your hair?" Oliver repeated, saying each word slowly.

"What?" Tamra grabbed her drink. "I do. It's a nice blue. And the spikes look good on him."

He chuckled and reached for his own drink.

"Was that bad?"

"No." He shook his head and took a sip of his drink. "And honestly, the way he was looking at you, I think he'd be happy with anything you say to him."

"You really think so?" She glanced back over her shoulder.

"Yep." Oliver tore a chunk off his croissant and popped it in his mouth.

"Hmm."

"What does that mean?"

"Nothing." She raised her cup to her lips.

"That was not a *nothing* hmm."

"So now you're an expert on hmms?"

"Defensive." He sucked on his straw.

"Do you think he's cute?"

Oliver subtly looked at the man now standing behind the counter. He couldn't be a day over twenty-five, he was rail thin, had gauges in both ears, tattoos on both arms, and, as Tamra pointed out, he had blue hair. "He's not my type but yes."

"What's your type?" she asked, leaning forward.

"I don't know." He ate the last of his croissant and pulled up a mental image of Jaime. "Darker hair with a little bit of salt right here"—he pointed to his own sideburns—"green eyes. Taller and broader, and more, um, conservative-looking?"

"Wow." She rubbed her lips together and smirked. "That is a very specific type." She took a drink. "*Very* specific."

It really was. His neck heated, and he occupied himself with his drink, hoping she'd move on.

"Well, he is totes my type."

He sighed in relief and flicked his gaze up. "Yeah?"

"Yep." She nibbled on her lip piercing. "You really think he's interested in me?"

One of the things Oliver most admired about Tamra was her inner strength and tenacity. He didn't like seeing her insecure.

"I know he is."

She sat up straight and smiled. "Awesome. Maybe I'll ask him out." She ate a piece of her muffin. "How about you? Are you dating anyone?"

He should have known he wasn't going to get away without talking about his too-specific type description.

"Sort of," he admitted, swirling the ice in his empty cup as a distraction from the uncomfortable conversation. Part of him very much wanted to talk about Jaime, both to brag and to get advice. But he was way too embarrassed to tell Tamra, or anyone, how they met and what Jaime did for a living.

"Is that all you're going to tell me?"

"He's great." He twisted his straw around. "Really, really great." Suddenly he had an idea of how to get Tamra's opinion without admitting anything. "Hey, have you seen that movie *Pretty Woman*?"

"So we're changing the topic?" When he didn't respond, she sighed and said, "Okay fine. Yes, I've seen it."

"Do you think it's realistic?"

"Which part?" She furrowed her brow and then said, "Never mind. Doesn't matter what your answer is. It's not realistic."

"Right." Oliver pulled his straw up and down. "A prostitute wouldn't actually fall in love with a client."

"Umm, she would if he's a bazillionaire who looks like Richard Gere! Julia Roberts falling for him is the most realistic part of that movie. But in real life, I seriously doubt a successful society guy would marry a hooker, even if she is drop-dead gorgeous and has a heart of gold."

Having first-hand experience with a drop-dead gorgeous, heart of gold escort, Oliver disagreed with Tamra's conclusion. "But if he wanted to be with her, you think she'd do it?"

"Richard. Gere." Tamra emphasized each word. "Next thing you'll ask is if I think Demi Moore would have slept with Robert Redford for a million dollars."

"Huh?"

"It's another old movie." She shook her head. "Never mind. Hey, you into *Warcraft*?"

"Uh-huh."

"We lost one of the people in our clan." She curled both hands around her cup and raised it to her mouth. "If you're interested, you can take his place."

"Seriously?"

"Yep."

"That'd be great." Oliver had always hopped into games with strangers, but he'd rather be part of a set group.

"Cool. We're WoWing tonight at seven thirty. Text me your handle."

" 'Kay." Oliver took out his phone, tapped in his information, and sent it to Tamra. "Done." From the corner of his eye, he noticed the barista looking their way. "He's staring at you again."

Tamra stood, straightened her shirt, flung her purse over her shoulder, and said, "I'm going in. Wish me luck."

Chapter 11

"WHAT TIME SHOULD I pick you up tonight?" Jaime sent the text and grinned as he waited to see how Oliver would respond.

"You're picking me up?"

"It's Friday. That's our standing date night." Which was a pattern they had fallen into with no discussion or planning. Other than the elephant-sized misunderstanding that Jaime intended to clear up that night, things between them were exceptionally easy.

"You don't usually pick me up."

"True. That means I need your address." Before Oliver could respond, Jaime texted again. "Also, pack a bag."

If Jaime didn't know Oliver, he may have thought he was being too presumptuous or pushing too hard. But Oliver appreciated having him take charge. Maybe someday he would be more confident, but until then, Jaime didn't mind steering the ship.

"Why am I packing a bag?"

"Because you're staying with me for the weekend."

"You don't already have plans this weekend?"

He hoped to be going to Kevin Rodley's Halloween party with Oliver as his date, but saying that via text would send Oliver into a tailspin.

"My plan is to spend the weekend with you." Truthful but not complete, which pretty much described Jaime's entire communication strategy with Oliver.

"*I seem to have forgotten the conversation where we agreed to this.*"

Even through text, Jaime could hear Oliver's playfully sarcastic tone and see him trying to frown but grinning instead.

"*No conversation. I made an executive decision.*"

"*How about 7? That way I have time to pack and eat.*"

"*6:30 and I'll feed you.*"

When the next text popped up, Jaime smiled broadly—it was an address in Madrona. Then his phone dinged again. "*You're a skilled negotiator.*"

"*So I've been told.*"

Negotiations were a key part of Jaime's job, but so far, getting on the same page with Oliver hadn't taken much skill, partly because Oliver was so easygoing and partly because they ultimately wanted the same things. Getting Oliver to agree to attend Kevin's party would probably be a challenge, but Jaime was willing to back down if it truly was something Oliver didn't want to do. He could reconnect with his old friends another time. Still, he'd try to talk Oliver into it because his friends were good guys and Oliver wanted to meet people in Seattle, and because he wanted Oliver to become a bigger part of his life, which would inevitably involve meeting his friends.

At a quarter after six, he parked his car in front of a nicely maintained gray and green wood-paneled house. The three-story had probably been one home at some point but someone had converted it into apartments, something that was happening more and more as Seattle rents continued rising. If anyone would expect an early arrival, it would be Oliver, but Jaime still texted him before he got out of the car.

"*I'm here. Just wanted to warn you in case you're naked.*"

He stepped out of the car and closed the door before his phone buzzed in his hand.

"*I'm dressed.*"

"*Too bad.*" He walked to the side of the house where he saw Oliver's apartment number.

"*Haha. I'll come out.*"

"*I'm almost at your door.*" Two more steps and he was knocking.

"Hey." Oliver pulled the door open. "You didn't have to get out of your car."

"I'm trying to court you. That means I need to come to your door instead of laying on the horn and yelling your name out the window." He stepped forward, wrapped his left arm around Oliver's waist, cupped his cheek with his right hand, and leaned forward. "It also means I need to give you a hello kiss." He closed the distance between them and brushed his lips against Oliver's. After the first gentle kiss, he delivered another and then another until Oliver parted his lips on a sigh, and then Jaime flicked his tongue over Oliver's mouth and pulled away.

Jaime looked at the handsome picture Oliver made—eyes closed, cheeks red, mouth slightly open. "Hi," he whispered.

Eyelids fluttering, Oliver rasped, "Hi." He licked his lips. "I'll get my bag and we can go."

He turned around and walked inside, Jaime behind him. "This place is cute." Gray paint in a lighter color than the outside, dinged but functional wood floors, a brown futon, and a square wood table with matching chairs.

"It's not fancy but rent in Seattle is so high it's the best I can afford. Only seven hundred square feet and I pay sixteen hundred a month." He stepped through the sole doorway in the open room, and Jaime followed him into a small bedroom with a neatly made queen bed and a single nightstand. "At least it comes furnished."

"Housing costs are crazy," Jaime agreed. "When I moved to Seattle, it wasn't like this."

"When was that?"

"Um, let's see." He had graduated from the University of Illinois with his computer engineering degree at the same time Jack had gotten his master's, and after a two-year pit stop in San Francisco, they had moved to Seattle and started a small company that eventually became Snow Storm. "Fifteen, almost sixteen years."

"Wow. That's a long time." Oliver picked up a duffle bag and flung it over his shoulder. "I was like in middle school then."

Jaime started coughing. When he caught his breath, he glared at Oliver, who was smiling so widely his cheeks had to hurt.

"Sorry, not sorry."

"Smartass," Jaime grumbled.

"That was fun."

He couldn't be mad at Oliver being comfortable enough to tease him. But he could fluster him right back. "You have what you need for work on Monday?"

"Monday?" Oliver stumbled in the doorway and then turned around.

"You're spending the weekend with me, remember?"

"I know you said that, but—" He gulped. "I thought you meant tonight and maybe tomorrow morning because you, uh, probably have plans Saturday night."

"I meant all weekend."

"Are you sure?" The hesitancy was back.

"Positive. I want to spend time with you."

He could see Oliver's anxiety but he could also see his longing. As it had at every turn, the latter won out.

"Okay. Give me a minute to get some more clothes." Oliver shuffled over to the closet and began rifling through it. "Wait." He turned around. "If I go with you, how will I get to work on Monday?"

"I'll take you. I have to be in Bellevue anyway."

There were always things he could do at the office, he just usually found work-arounds so he would stay out of Jack's space. But they'd truly turned a corner now, and he no longer thought Jack would be bothered by his presence.

"Really?"

Nodding, Jaime said, "And my house is a little closer to your office so we'll cut your commute time."

"I tried to find an apartment by Snow Storm but there was no way I could swing the rent in Bellevue. Thankfully they're super accommodating and unless we have a meeting or something, I either drive in early and leave before rush hour or come in late and stay until most people are off the road." Oliver zipped his bag, closed his closet door, and turned back around. "But I really like my job so usually I come in early *and* stay late so traffic isn't an issue."

"You're a dream employee. I bet they love you."

"I'm the new guy so I barely know anyone." They walked to the front door and out of the apartment together. "Where do you live?" Oliver asked as he locked up.

"Laurelhurst."

Forehead crinkling, Oliver said, "Where is that? I don't know all the neighborhoods yet."

"Little bit north of here." Jaime put his hand on Oliver's

back and walked him to the car. "You'll like it."

The doors unlocked when they approached and they both got inside.

"Toss your bag in the backseat," Jaime said.

"Holy crap. This is a Model S."

He turned to the side to see a slack-jawed Oliver darting his gaze all over the car.

"Yes." He took the duffle bag from Oliver's lap, twisted to the side, and set it in the back. "Buckle up."

"You drive a Tesla." Oliver pulled on his seatbelt, using what Jaime assumed was muscle memory because his brain was clearly otherwise occupied.

"Yes."

There were a few moments of silence as Jaime pulled away from the curb and began the drive to his house.

"This is my exact car in *Sims* except mine's silver."

"Really? You can drive it tomorrow, if you want."

"Seriously?" Oliver asked, sounding awed.

Pleased he could make Oliver happy, especially because he knew there would be some decidedly unhappy moments coming right up, Jaime said, "Yes."

"Is this your friend's car? The one you were dog sitting for?"

Not looking away from the road, he said, "Nope."

Another few minutes passed before Oliver asked, "Another friend?"

"No." He could visualize Oliver's mental wheels turning.

More silence and then, "This is your car?"

Jaime nodded.

This time Oliver stayed quiet for longer before saying, "There is no way anyone could afford a car like this getting paid fifty dollars an hour. No way." Apparently he had used his time to perform mental calculations.

"You're definitely right about that."

If Oliver's speak-think-speak pattern held, they'd be pulling up to Jaime's house at around the time Oliver figured out what to say next. Seeing where Jaime lived would surely bring with it a new slew of questions, but rather than trying to avoid them like he had for the past month and a half, Jaime wanted to be open with Oliver about who he was and who he wasn't. He was certain Oliver was ready. Plus, Oliver didn't have his car, so even if he did freak out, he wouldn't be able to leave without calling for a ride, and Jaime was confident he could calm him down enough to stay in the time it would take an Uber to arrive.

"So you don't do this job for the money?"

Turning his head to the right, Jaime made eye contact with Oliver. "Nothing I've done with you has been for money. Not one thing." He returned his focus to the road. "I meant what I said—I enjoy being with you and I want more of that. A lot more."

"So this is what? A hobby? A kink?" Oliver looked away, bit his lip, and tugged at the seam on the side of his pants. "I don't understand."

"We're here. Let's go inside and talk."

Oliver squinted as he leaned forward to look out the windshield. In the daylight, he would have seen lush bushes, brick walls, and behind them, the tops of large homes. But the neighborhood didn't have many streetlights and it was hard to make much out in the dark.

"We can take the dogs for a walk tomorrow and you'll be able to see everything." Turning onto his gray stone driveway, Jaime touched the screen in the center console and slowed down while he waited for his garage door to roll up.

"Sorry. I was…" Oliver sighed. "I guess I was trying to learn more about you."

"Nothing to be sorry about." He drove into the garage and then touched the screen to close it. "I'll tell you anything you want to know." Just as Jaime grabbed the door handle, Oliver wrapped his hand around Jaime's arm, so instead of leaving the car, Jaime twisted his head to the side.

"I've wanted to get to know you better, to ask all sorts of details, but I haven't felt like I had the right to pry." Oliver chewed on the corner of his lip. "I'm not a client anymore, right?"

Jaime reached his hand forward and swiped his thumb over Oliver's lip. "You were never a client. That's one of the things we need to talk about."

Swallowing hard, Oliver nodded, and then he took a deep breath and got out of the car. When Oliver opened the back door and retrieved his bag, Jaime sighed in relief. If Oliver had the presence of mind to remember his things, he wasn't paralyzed by his nerves, and if he was bringing his clothes inside, he hadn't changed his mind about staying with Jaime.

After opening the door into the house, Jaime waited for Oliver to catch up to him and then he placed his hand on Oliver's back and led him inside. Two tiny whirlwinds immediately greeted them.

"Hi, girls." Jaime dropped to his haunches and petted his two pups. "Do you remember Oliver?"

"Kiki and Lulu, right?" Oliver's bag hit the ground and then he sat down beside Jaime and reached for the dogs. Kiki crawled onto his lap. "Aww, you remember me, don't you? Such a sweetheart."

After a few minutes of love, the dogs got bored and ran off.

133

"You ready for a tour?" Jaime asked. He stood and held his hand out to Oliver.

"Sure." Oliver grabbed onto his hand, pulled himself up, and then lifted his bag off the floor.

"Kitchen first," Jaime said. "I need to heat the food." They walked down the short hallway, past the doors to the laundry room and storage room, and into the eat-in kitchen.

"Wow." Oliver turned in a circle, looking around. "This house is incredible."

"Thank you." Jaime reached for Oliver's bag.

"You must be crazy rich." He reared back, as if surprised by his own comment, and then his cheeks reddened. "Sorry. That was rude."

"It was true. And I'm not offended. I've been incredibly lucky in life." He gently tugged the bag out of Oliver's hands. "My parents paid for my education, so I was able to focus on my classes without worrying about a job. When I graduated, I wasn't burdened by student debt, and I knew my parents were there as a safety net, so I had the luxury of taking risks with my career choices."

"This house is straight out of a posh game map." Oliver dragged his hand over the square ebony table as he stepped over to the picture window that took up a whole wall. Nearly the entire back of the house was made of glass, so most rooms had a great view of Lake Washington. "Guess your risks paid off."

"They have." Jaime walked over to the oven and put it on warm. "One of my favorite inspirational quotes is by Wayne Gretzky: you miss a hundred percent of the shots you don't take. If I see an opening, I take the shot." Jaime turned around and waited for Oliver to meet his gaze before saying, "Both in my professional life and my personal one."

"Why do I get the feeling you're trying to tell me something?" Oliver asked, frowning.

"Because I am." He flung Oliver's bag over his shoulder. "I had dinner delivered earlier and I just put the oven on warm. Let's put your things away." He walked through the kitchen to the opening leading into the main living area. "I'll give you a little tour on the way to the bedroom."

"Are you going to elaborate on that risk thing or is cryptic the name of the game tonight?"

"I'll elaborate." The house was built to optimize the views so the hallway ran along the front and all of the rooms were situated along the back with picture windows showing the lake. "That's the living room and dining room." He pointed to their left at the open space that took up nearly half of the bottom floor. "The back wall that looks like huge windows is actually sets of sliding doors. The patio is at the exact same level as the inside, so when the weather's nice, we can open the doors and have one big space. I've hosted events with more than two hundred fifty people, and we weren't crowded."

"It's a nice-looking space." Oliver followed behind him, his teeth working on his lip and his eyebrows drawn tightly together. Jaime knew he was gathering information and slotting it together in his mind. "This is the family room, but I live here alone, so to me, it's the room where I have comfortable furniture. When people come over, this is where we hang out. Well, this and the kitchen." They reached an area where the hallway widened and Jaime pointed ahead. "There's a guest room, bathroom, and office down there. If someone stays with me, they can use that space and have privacy. Other than that, I don't go down there." He stepped toward the stairs. "The people who built this house put in an elevator, but I never use it." He climbed the stairs, waited for Oliver on the landing and pointed in the same direction he had when they were on the first floor. "There are two bedrooms that way, each with a bathroom. I'm not sure I've stepped foot in them since I toured the house. I didn't even bother with furniture."

"Why did you get a house this big if you don't need it?"

"I liked the location. Loved the lot. It's about twice the size of anything else in the neighborhood, all of it lakefront. And I needed something that would work well for entertaining." He led them toward his bedroom, pointing at each door as he passed it. "Two offices here, side by side with a barn door separating them. Workout room." He smiled at Jaime. "If I'm home and I'm not sleeping or working, I end up in there." He opened the double doors at the end of the hall. "This is my bedroom." The wall directly opposite them ended three quarters of the way across the room. "There's a bathroom, second laundry room, and closet this way." He walked into the closet. "It's built for two and there's only one of me, so there's plenty of space for you to hang up your things." He took a deep breath and turned around, putting him a breath's distance from Oliver. "Take as much time as you need." He leaned forward and brushed his lips over Oliver's. "I'll wait for you in the bedroom."

The time alone in the closet was designed to give an overwhelmed Oliver space and privacy. In planning for the night, Jaime had gone over what he would say and when he would say it. He had prepared himself for what he thought would be any possible reaction from Oliver, and he felt ready to apologize, to seduce, to joke, to basically do anything to calm what he expected would be an embarrassed and anxious to the point of panic man. But moments after Jaime settled into one of the two overstuffed armchairs facing the fireplace in the corner of his room, a calm-looking Oliver came in.

"I'm telling myself this was all a huge coincidence and not the most involved and cruel haze-the-new-guy prank ever."

Jaime was so used to the things his made-up Oliver would say, that he had trouble following what the real life version meant.

"I'm standing here, thinking back to every conversation we had." Oliver leaned against the wall on the opposite side of the room. "I don't think I told you where I worked until last weekend, so I guess there's plausible deniability there. But the first time we met, you saw my book, the coding book, so you knew I knew who you were. Sort of."

Paradoxically, Oliver's even tone and blank expression did what the hysteria Jaime had prepared for could not: it made his heart race and sent his lungs into overdrive.

"How did you figure it out?" The second he heard his own words, he kicked himself for his phrasing. He had sounded like he was trying to hide the information from Oliver, which was the opposite of the truth. "Never mind. I—"

"There are built-in bookcases in every room in your house and you get a lot of awards."

When he and Jack had broken up, Jaime had taken his clothes, his childhood pictures, and a painting his grandfather left him when he passed away. Everything else, he had left for Jack. In the past eight years, he had accumulated some art and knickknacks, but not enough to fill the many shelves in the house, so when Snow Storm received a paperweight or statue or other corporate version of a trophy, he set it on one of his shelves and forgot about it. Same with photographs from charity golf tournaments and awards banquets.

"I walk by those every day, so I don't even see them anymore." Worried, Jaime stood, intending to bridge the distance between them.

Oliver held his hand out, indicating that Jaime should stay where he was. "Were you going to tell me?"

"Yes. That's one of the reasons I wanted you to come over tonight."

"Okay." Oliver dragged a trembling hand through his hair, and Jaime realized he was more affected than he was showing. "Okay."

"Come sit with me." Jaime lowered himself back into his seat and pointed to the empty armchair beside him.

After a few interminable seconds, Oliver walked over. He slid his palm over the back of the chair and hesitated.

"This isn't going at all like it did in my head," Jaime admitted.

Oliver arched his eyebrows.

"I had it all scripted. My lines. Your lines. The whole thing. But I didn't account for"—he took a deep breath and shook his head—"eyesight." All his careful plans, blown away because he couldn't remember to put away a few decorations. He laughed at the ridiculousness of the situation. "Please sit down, baby."

With a dip of his chin, Oliver stepped around the chair and perched on the edge. "There's no way you could have known I'd call that escort ad, so you didn't set me up as part of some employment check or whatever."

"I absolutely did not set you up. Like you said, I didn't know you worked for Snow Storm until last weekend."

"Yeah." Oliver nodded. "What I've been able to piece together so far is that you're not like a *Tomb Raider* level boss who's out to mess me up for sport, but you get paid to have sex, and it's not because you need the money. So is this something that turns you on? Like a kink?"

"You're right that I'm not a villain but I'm also not nearly that exciting." Jaime propped his forearms on his knees, threaded his hands together, and cleared his throat. "The night we met, I had plans to hang out with a group of friends at the Bookstore. My dinner meeting in Pioneer Square ended early but not so early that I had time to do anything else, so I went to the bar, planning to wait for my friends. Instead, I ran into the most gorgeous guy I'd seen in as long as I could remember and he was holding a textbook I wrote in my coding days." He smiled at the memory. "If that wasn't a sign that you were the perfect man for me, I don't know what would have been, so I approached you. I planned to flirt, buy you a drink, see if there was any interest but then—"

"Oh my God. I'm so embarrassed." Oliver squeezed his eyes shut. "You're basically my boss and I called you a prostitute."

"No." Jaime leaned over and put his hand on Oliver's thigh. "Don't be embarrassed. I thought you were so sweet. So genuine. I don't meet people like you, ever. And when you shared your history and your worries with me...I knew if I told you the truth, I'd never have a chance because you'd get scared and leave. And, oh man, I did *not* want you to leave." Jaime shook his head and blew out a harsh breath. "I figured I could do what you were hiring someone to do, so I got us out of the bar before the real escort got there, and in my head I was thinking, 'no harm, no foul.' But then..."

"But then?"

"Then I spent more time with you." Jaime shrugged. "Sometimes a guy's good-looking but you get into bed and there's no chemistry. With you, it was combustible. I couldn't walk away from a chance at seeing you again. And then again. And then again. Somewhere along the way I realized we fit really well together and I wanted more than a few hours a week in bed with you, which meant coming clean." Jaime took a deep breath and met Oliver's gaze. "So now we're here."

Chapter 12

OLIVER LEANED HIS head against the back of the armchair, closed his eyes, and considered everything he had learned in the past hour.

If he had been in this situation two months ago, he would have been riddled with anxiety and his brain would have been coming up with all the ways he would ruin things and drive Jaime away. Or, more accurately, two months ago he would have never leveled up enough to be in this situation because he wouldn't have had the nerve to talk with a guy who looked like Jaime; he probably wouldn't have even had the nerve to *look* at a guy who looked like Jaime. The only reason he was there now was because he had thought Jaime wanted what he could give—payment.

"Tell me what you're thinking."

Slowly opening his eyes, Oliver focused on Jaime. He was leaning forward, hands clasped together, forehead crinkled, and jaw ticcing. If he had been holding up an iPad with the word "worried" flashing on the screen, his feelings wouldn't have been clearer.

"I'm not mad. I just…needed to hit the pause button for a sec." He had to take a break from talking and seeing and hearing so he could think. "I understand why you did what you did. I wish I wasn't so…whatever it is I am that makes me act like a complete idiot around guys. I'm embarrassed that you know how pathetic and desperate I am."

"You've never been pathetic, and if you were desperate before, you're definitely not now." Jaime gave him a pointed look.

"I can't even…" Oliver couldn't help it, he laughed. His eyes felt wet, but he ignored that and focused on breathing. "You've been lying to me from the beginning. You tricked me into telling you my biggest secrets. You can destroy my career in a flash. But you're offended because I said I was acting desperate and somehow that's a reflection on you?"

"Yes. Pretty much."

"You're not supposed to agree with someone who's throwing shade." Oliver wiped the back of his hands over his eyes.

"I'd be more upset if I thought you meant *most* of that."

"I know you didn't trick me, but I'm pretty on fleek with the rest of it."

"On what?"

"It means I'm on point." Oliver sniffled and swiped at his eyes again. "And you're old."

"Thanks."

"I guess I should just be happy to save all that time I was spending on Reddit researching whether prostitutes fall in love with their clients."

Jaime snorted. "Did you really do that?"

"Absolutely not," Oliver said while nodding. "So you seriously came up to me at the Bookstore because you were interested?"

"Very interested." Jaime's voice lowered and his eyes bore into Oliver.

"It's hard for me to understand that because…look at you." He pointed at Jaime. "And look at me."

"I love looking at you. Love touching you too. Remember

what I told you last week?"

He did remember, but he wanted to hear it again. Needed to hear it again. "I was drinking that night so my recollection of events is a little fuzzy. Maybe you should jog my memory?"

Jaime stood, stepped over to Oliver, and straddled him. "Let's see." He threaded his fingers through Oliver's hair. "I believe what I said was that your body turns me on. Your size, your chest hair, your ass." Jaime leaned forward, brushed his lips over Oliver's, and whispered, "Everything about you is sexy to me."

Instinctively, Oliver's lips parted and his eyes closed. He clung to Jaime's shoulders and moaned quietly when Jaime kissed him again, open-mouthed that time. They continued connecting, lips and tongues tasting and touching, heads tilting to one side and then the other, torsos rubbing and grinding. Breathless, they eventually separated, but Jaime rested his forehead against Oliver's, as if he wanted to stay close.

"I hope you'll eventually see yourself the way I see you." Jaime grazed his lips across Oliver's jaw and down his neck. "Not that I mind the process of reminding you how I feel."

"I don't mind it either." Hands twitching, Oliver squeezed and released Jaime's muscled arms.

"Our dinner's sure to be warm by now." Jaime caressed Oliver's cheek. "Are you hungry?"

"Yeah." Oliver rested his head against Jaime's chest and sighed when Jaime gently combed his fingers through his hair. "It seems like I should be freaking out right now, but I'm not." In fact, he felt more secure about Jaime's feelings than he had before he found out who Jaime actually was and who he wasn't.

"That's a good thing." Jaime kissed Oliver's forehead and then climbed off his lap and held his hand out.

"I reserve the right to have a breakdown later," Oliver said, taking his hand and standing.

"Deal." Jaime smiled and walked out of the room, keeping Oliver's hand in his own. "You know what I wonder?"

"What?"

"What happened to the escort you called."

"Huh." Oliver blinked. "I didn't think of that."

"You've known I wasn't him for all of a half hour. I've had more time to ponder." They reached the staircase, so Jaime released his hand, waited for him to go ahead, and then followed. "That first night, I gave you my number to set up more appointments, but I always had a niggling worry that he'd try to get in touch with you."

"No." Oliver shook his head. "I called the number in the ad and set up a time and place to meet. That was it. They don't have my contact info."

"Lucky me." They reached the bottom of the stairs and Jaime smiled softly at him. "His loss was definitely my gain."

Not sure how to respond to the sweet words, Oliver changed the topic. "How was your day?"

"Busy. I'm juggling too many projects right now so it seems like I spend half my time deciding what I can push to the next day."

"That's probably not the most efficient use of your time."

"No, it's really not." The dogs trotted up to them, and Jaime squatted down to give them quick pets. "What about you? Good day?"

"Uh-huh. Work was good. On the way home, I found a chicken nugget wedged in the seat of my car, which is a total Easter egg. I made out with a hot guy. And now I'm about to eat dinner." He grinned. "Totally hit my bonus round today."

Rising, Jaime said, "Don't tell me you ate something that's been in your car for who knows how long."

"Okay, I won't, and I'd put the odds at like eighty-three percent that the nugget is from lunch yesterday."

"Eighty-three percent?" Jaime repeated, sounding amused.

"Maybe eighty-two-point-five."

Jaime laughed. "Well, when you put it that way, it really is your lucky day. Maybe you should buy a lottery ticket."

"Yep."

As they walked into the kitchen, Jaime pointed at the over-sized refrigerator. "Drinks are in the fridge. I'll get the food out of the oven." He donned a pair of silicone oven mitts, opened one of the two wall-ovens, and began removing foil takeout containers. "What numbers do you play?"

"Numbers?"

"In the lottery. Are your numbers birthdays or memorable events or something else?"

"When I play, I do the random numbers." Oliver pulled the heavy refrigerator door open and inventoried the beverage options. "Water, beer, iced tea, or the tiniest pop of all time?"

"Tea please. Doesn't matter which flavor. Why don't you use lucky numbers?"

"Because I'm not a regular lotto player, and if I use the same numbers every time, it's inevitable that those numbers will win on a week I haven't bought a ticket. I can't deal with knowing I should have won but not actually winning." He fake shuddered. "Horror."

"You're hilarious." Jaime smiled at him as he set the food on the huge butcher-block island. "And adorable."

Nobody had ever looked at Oliver quite like that and it made him shuffle from foot to foot uncomfortably. "I'm not mad; you don't have to be so nice to me."

"Hey." Jaime walked over to him and curled his mitted-hand around Oliver's nape. "I know you're not mad, which shows how amazing you are because most people would have handed me my nuts before calming down. This isn't me putting on a show. I'm just really glad you're here with me."

He was in a real life version of a fantasy and he had to keep poking at it to see if it'd pop. "My default setting seems to be putting my foot in my mouth."

"The way we met was...*unconventional* and you've had a lot of information to process in a short time." Jaime kissed his forehead, stepped back, and then looked at his own hand. "And I'm still wearing these oven mitts."

"I know." Oliver laughed. "We're both coming apart at the seams. It's time for a reload. What are we eating?"

"Indian food. Do you like it?"

"Love it. But there's not much I don't like. As my mother always says, I'm a good eater."

"What you are is sensuous." Jaime took two plates out of the smooth walnut cabinets and began dishing out food. "Being with someone who takes so much pleasure in things is—" Jaime gulped and looked at Oliver, his gaze heated. "You're incredibly sexy."

Trying not to fidget like a small child, Oliver mumbled, "I don't know how to respond when you say things like that."

"No response needed." Jaime pulled silverware out of the drawer, set it on the plates, and then carried them to the kitchen table. "Oh. Listen to this awkward slash funny story from today."

The promise of a change in topic relaxed Oliver. Shoulders loosening, he picked up the drinks and walked to the table.

"I was at a business lunch with a man who recently had his first child. He's my age so it's a little later in life than usual and he's uber proud, so he whipped out his phone and showed everyone pictures. I was at the opposite end of the table and I couldn't see anything but I did the polite nod and oohed and aahed and that was that. Well, at least I thought that was that. I happened to be parked next to him, and when we got to our cars, he said he forgot to show us his favorite picture and then he shoved his phone in my face. I swear to you, I jumped back and gasped. That was the most ugly baby I have ever seen. I smoothed things over by saying he took me off guard because I'm sensitive to fast movements but, man." Jaime shook his head. "We have another meeting in a couple of weeks and he's bound to have more pictures, so I'll have to be ready with something flattering to say about his ugly baby." He forked a piece of chicken and raised it to his mouth. "I have no idea what that can be when all I have to work with is the visual proof of what happens when oil gene pools mix with water gene pools."

Oliver laughed, partly because of the animated way Jaime relayed the story and partly because he was relieved to be talking about something light. "Back home when someone has an ugly baby, we say, 'Aww, look how alert he is!'" He scooped some saag paneer onto his fork and took a bite.

"Alert is a compliment?"

"Seems like people enjoy hearing it." Oliver twisted his lips to the side. "I have no clue why." He took another bite. "Same with the head-shape thing."

"Head shape?"

"Uh-huh." Oliver swallowed his food and picked up his water bottle. "Oh, your baby's head is such a wonderful shape!" He pressed the bottle to his mouth and took a drink. "This is delicious."

"You've heard people compliment a baby's head?"

"All the time." He tore a piece off his naan. "I have a big extended family and most of my cousins have kids. The head thing is huge."

"So is this baby's."

Oliver raised his eyebrows in question.

"Big and"—Jaime brought his hands up to either side of his head and moved them around—"oddly shaped."

"Maybe you'd better stick to the 'alert' thing."

"Good idea. Hopefully he won't pull up a picture of the baby asleep."

"If he does, you can compliment him on his baby being a good sleeper. People love that one."

"People are odd about their children."

"Yeah." Oliver scooped up potatoes and cauliflower. "Do you want to have kids?" He put the food in his mouth, realized how that question sounded, and almost choked. "Not with me." He forced himself to swallow, coughed, and then quickly grabbed for his water bottle. "I mean like theoretical kids," he rasped. He gulped down his water, tapped his fist against his chest, and cleared his throat. "Like in theory."

"Theoretical kids in theory?" Jaime asked. His amused tone gave Oliver the courage to make eye contact. "Remind me how those differ from theoretical kids in actuality. Or is it actual kids in theory? Or maybe actual kids in actuality?" Jaime shook his head and pursed his lips, looking serious even though he clearly wasn't. "It's all very complicated."

"Stop being mean."

"Okay." Jaime chuckled. "Do I want to have kids? Well, when I was younger, I was busy having fun and making my way in the world so I never thought about having children. Then when I was…" He furrowed his brow, looking thoughtful. "About twenty-nine or thirty, so around your age, I started wondering what having a family would be like but—" He cringed, his words coming to a halt and his expression nearly haunted.

"What?" Oliver asked, concerned about Jaime's sudden mood change.

"Are we doing this relationship thing?"

"Doing this relationship thing?" Oliver repeated, saying each word slowly.

"I'm attracted to you. I love being with you. I admire your intelligence and your spirit and your heart. You're what I've always wanted but couldn't find, all wrapped up in a package so sexy it's hard for me to concentrate." Jaime let out a deep breath. "That's it. I've laid my cards on the table." He looked at Oliver expectantly. "Your turn."

By the time Jaime was done talking, Oliver's heart was slamming against his ribcage. "I…" He licked his lips and tried to control his breathing. "Okay, no freaking out." He drew in air through his nose and let it out through his mouth. "I'm not freaking out."

"Your announcement makes that very clear." Jaime tilted one side of his mouth up.

"I didn't mean to say that out loud." Oliver wiped his clammy palms on his pants. "I was just—"

"*Not* freaking out?" Jaime supplied.

The teasing helped put things in perspective. "Okay." Oliver chuckled at his own foolishness. "It's possible I'm freaking out a little, but that's only because you're like my dream guy and you said…" He shook his head. "But you're talking about dating, which is basically what we've been doing, right? I mean, it's not as if you declared your undying love or anything."

Staying silent, Jaime looked at Oliver meaningfully and arched his eyebrows. Whether that meant he was questioning the reason for Oliver's actions, the description of them having dated, or the comment about his undying love, Oliver didn't know and he was too afraid to ask.

"So, uh," Oliver continued. "My cards are that I want to date you and"—he cleared his throat—"have a relationship with you."

"I'm glad we're on the same page." Jaime paused and grinned. "Mostly."

"Good." Oliver sighed, fiddled with his fork, and then looked at Jaime. "What were we talking about?"

"Past relationships."

"I only had the one sort of relationship and you know how it ended." Quickly and embarrassingly.

"That guy, whoever he is, has horrible judgment."

"Maybe we just weren't right for each other."

"I'm glad to hear you say that." Jaime pushed his plate aside, reached across the table, and gently curled his hand around Oliver's wrist. "It's much better than assuming there's something wrong with you. Especially when there very much isn't."

Oliver nodded, wondering when he had stopped considering himself at fault for the end of his one and only relationship and instead chalked it up to being a bad match. After he started spending time with Jaime, that was when.

"Thank you for helping me see that." Oliver slipped his hand into Jaime's.

"What kind of boyfriend would I be if I didn't constantly tell you how great you are in bed?"

Dipping his chin, Oliver smiled at Jaime's choice of title. "You're an amazing boyfriend." He looked at Jaime from underneath his lashes. "And I can be too. Please be patient with me while I figure it out?"

"I don't usually sweat the small stuff, but even if I did, there'd be nothing for you to figure out. You being yourself is what reeled me in."

"And there I was, not even knowing I was fishing."

"Sure you knew. Remember that night at the Bookstore? You asked me to go fishing with you." Jaime waggled his eyebrows comically. "*Nekkid* fishing."

"Oh God." Oliver propped both elbows on the table and dropped his face into his hands. "Let's never speak of the dumb things I said."

"I found you utterly charming." Jaime combed his fingers through Oliver's hair. "Still do." He removed his hand and then silverware clanged against a plate.

Raising his head, Oliver said, "That night feels like a million years ago."

Fork hovering in front of his mouth, Jaime said, "It does, doesn't it?"

"Yeah."

"That's how I know this is right." Jaime popped the food into his mouth.

"What do you mean?"

After swallowing his food, Jaime set his fork down and said, "Being with you is as comfortable as it is exciting. It feels so right down deep that it's hard to remember you weren't always in my life." He picked up his tea bottle and picked at the label. "When someone's a bad match in every way, you figure it out on the first day. The ones who aren't bad but aren't great either, take two encounters, maybe three. The hard ones are people who *should* fit, the men who, on paper, are perfect for you, but something inside you says they're not the one. You can spend years with someone, wondering what the hell's wrong with you because he's everything you should want but..." Jaime pressed his lips together and shook his head. "You don't."

"It sort of sounds like you're describing a gay guy marrying the perfect girl and not wanting to admit why she isn't perfect for him."

"Maybe a little," Jaime conceded. "For me, it wasn't about hiding in the closet. My 'should have been perfect but wasn't' person is a man." Expression pained, he curled his hand around his bottle and shakily raised it to his lips.

"Are you talking about Jack Storm?" Oliver chewed on the corner of his lip. "I heard a rumor that the two of you used to be together or whatever."

"No whatever about it. Jack and I were a couple for ten years."

"That's a long time."

Jaime nodded. "When you're twenty-two at the beginning, it can feel like a lifetime."

Oliver shoved down an emotion he refused to characterize as jealousy. Everyone had exes. Maybe not ones that lasted ten years, but that was just time, right? He wished he could believe himself. "A person at work said you stopped being involved with Snow Storm because of the breakup. Was it...bad?"

"I'm still very much involved in the company. I did change my role to keep myself away from the office and day-to-day operations, but not because Jack and I can't stand each other." Jaime looked out the large window. "Getting along was never our problem."

The emotion was definitely jealousy. "Am I allowed to ask what happened?"

"There aren't lines in the sand, Oliver. You can ask me anything. But this one's hard to explain." He scratched the back of his left hand. "I had a hard time understanding it myself."

Part of Oliver wanted to yell at Jaime to get on with his explanation and another part wanted to throw his hand up and tell Jaime to never bring up his ex again. He did neither.

"You'll meet Jack and see that he's wonderful." Jaime smiled, but his expression wasn't happy. "He's a good person. Smart, driven, loyal. We're close to the same age, both of us grew up outside of Chicago, we were both interested in getting into the tech industry, both gay. It should have been a perfect match, and for Jack, I think it was." He finally turned away from the window and looked at Oliver. "Or it would have been if I'd felt the way about him as I do about you."

"I don't know what that means," Oliver said, trying to stay calm. Jaime was sharing something personal and clearly painful. He needed to be supportive instead of selfishly focusing on his own insecurities.

"When I saw you that first time, my heart started beating faster. The closer I got to you, the more my body reacted. It was visceral. Getting to know you has made that attraction stronger." As he spoke, Jaime's voice had gotten more animated, his expression happier, but then he crumpled again. "No matter how hard I tried, I couldn't feel that spark with Jack. Not ever." He was silent for a few seconds. "Eventually, I admitted to myself that it'd never happen and then I admitted it to him."

"How long ago was that?"

"Eight years." Jaime let out a deep breath and then twined his fingers with Oliver's. "You don't need to worry about this being a rebound."

"I wasn't." But only because he hadn't thought of it. "I was just curious." He rubbed his thumb back and forth across Jaime's palm and thought about all the information he'd just learned. "So you're forty?"

"Give you numbers, and your brain starts calculating." Jaime chuckled. "Yes, I'm forty."

"When's your birthday?"

"The day after Christmas. When's yours?"

"February third. I'll be twenty-nine."

"I'm sort of robbing the cradle, aren't I?"

"Maybe a little." Oliver smiled and then sighed. "Jaime?"

"Yes?" Jaime looked at him expectantly.

"Are you, uh, done with dinner?"

Furrowing his brow, Jaime said, "I can be."

"Me too." Oliver glanced down and then flicked his gaze back up. "I feel like I've hit the ceiling on revelations and deep conversations for the day and I just want to go to bed and be close to you."

Jaime pushed his chair back and gathered their dishes. "I'm on board with that plan."

Chapter 13

"I'M PRETTY SURE my eight-year-old nephew is allowed to stay up later than this." Oliver shifted from side to side, apparently having trouble finding a comfortable position.

"Well in our case, going to bed at nine o'clock is a treat." Jaime sat on the end of the mattress and waited for him to settle.

"That's so true." Oliver fluffed his pillow. "I used to whine and beg when my parents said it was bedtime. Now I'm like, 'Oh thank goodness I can finally go to sleep.'"

"I wasn't talking about sleep," Jaime said suggestively.

Oliver stopped straightening the blanket and stared at him.

"Are you done fidgeting?" he asked, amused.

"Uh-huh." Oliver bobbed his head and dropped his arms to his sides.

"Good." Jaime stood, tucked his thumbs into his waistband, and pushed his boxer briefs down. "You have room for me?"

Completely disregarding the effort he had put into getting the bedding just so, Oliver yanked the blanket back and exposed his nearly naked body. When Jaime had met him, Oliver had been ashamed of his appearance and self-conscious when he wasn't wearing clothes. But tonight, he had stripped down without hesitation and stood beside Jaime in his underwear while they brushed their teeth and washed up before bed. Jaime loved the new confidence as much as he loved the view.

"You're warm." Jaime climbed into the bed and curled himself around Oliver, his knee wedged between Oliver's thighs, his arm wrapped around Oliver's waist, and his head pillowed on Oliver's chest. "Mmm, feel so good." He kissed the side of Oliver's neck and tucked himself as close as possible.

"You feel good too," Oliver said, voice gravelly. He wound his arms around Jaime and caressed his back.

Engulfed by a thick, hot body, Jaime shivered. This had been his idea of the perfect way to go to sleep at night and wake up in the morning. So far, reality was surpassing his imagination.

"I already know you don't work in the Bellevue office so does that mean Snow Storm has another space somewhere for executives or do you work from here?"

"No other space." Jaime combed his fingers through Oliver's chest hair. "The home office I showed you has everything I need, but really, I spend more time in meetings than I do sitting at a desk. When I told you I host events here, it's almost always work-related. My focus is getting Snow Storm on every retail shelf—both physical and virtual—and in as many homes as possible. Distribution and marketing. That's what I do." He rubbed his knee against Oliver's leg, enjoying the texture of his hair. "We have outside consultants for some of it and I manage them. There are a half dozen people in the office who work under Jack and do a decent number of projects for me. But most of what I do is conversations and negotiations."

"So you're not stuck here alone all day?"

Of course, Oliver's first thought was about Jaime's wellbeing. "You're a sweetheart." Jaime leaned up and brushed his lips over Oliver's. "Don't worry about me being lonely at work. I almost never have a day without a meeting outside of the house, and even when I'm home, I'm usually on the phone. The only time I completely disconnect is when I'm working out. I have a personal rule that my cell doesn't come into the gym with me."

"That's a coincidence. I have that rule too." Oliver paused and his lips twitched. "I also have a rule where I don't go anywhere without my phone. I don't violate either of them."

It took Jaime a few seconds to follow and then he laughed. "Very clever."

"Very true."

"Didn't you tell me you were going to join a gym?" Jaime slid his hand down Oliver's chest and over his stomach. "Not that you need to lose weight. In fact, I hope you *don't* lose weight. But exercise keeps you healthy."

"Yeah, I know. I keep telling myself I'll do it, but literally anything else seems more appealing so I never get around to it."

"What don't you like about it?" Jaime shifted so he was lying on his stomach, looking up at Oliver's face.

"About the gym?"

"Yes." Jaime nodded.

"I don't know. It smells bad. A clean sweat odor, I like, but gyms smell closed-in and stuffy. The vinyl chairs are always slick from whoever used a machine before me. The towels they give you to wipe yourself are crusty and I never know if that's because they use industrial soap to wash them or if they skip the washing and what I'm feeling when I wipe my forehead is someone else's dried sweat."

"So it's not the exercise that bothers you, it's rubbing someone else's stink all over your face?"

"That and I feel out of place there." Oliver looked at a spot past Jaime's head. "Like they're all looking at me and laughing at the sweaty fat guy huffing and puffing in a room full of perfect bodies."

"There are all sorts of body types at the gym and we all have a different idea of perfect." Jaime dipped down and kissed his way across Oliver's stomach. "To me, for example, that's you." He enjoyed watching Oliver's blue and white striped boxers rise, the fabric pushed up by his hardening dick. "But if you don't like gyms and want to work out, I have a solution."

"What's that?" Oliver sounded slightly breathless.

"Come over here. I don't have the same equipment as the PRO Sports Club, but I have everything you need for decent cardio and strength training."

"You want me to work out at your house?"

"Among other things, yes." Jaime circled his fingertip around Oliver's nipple and watched it pebble.

"You know what's weird?"

"What?" Jaime shifted his attention to the other nipple.

"You invited me over to exercise, and I immediately started thinking about what that meant, and if it was too soon to be so serious and yet I came here tonight knowing we'd be having sex."

"I'm not following." Jaime scrunched his eyebrows together. "Do you want to slow things down?"

"No!" Oliver's tone was flatteringly emphatic. "Not that I want to crowd you or cling or do whatever it is people find off-putting."

"I'm well and truly lost," Jaime admitted. "Are you saying working out here is too serious or are you worried I'll think you're moving too fast?" Jaime paused. "Because I won't."

"Neither." Oliver shook his head. "I was making a point. Well, *trying* to make a point. Clearly, I didn't succeed."

"Try again." Jaime scooted up and laid his head on the pillow, bringing him eye-to-eye with Oliver. "I'll focus harder this time."

"It's not all that interesting. I was just pointing out how we accept invitations for sex without a second thought, but we consider normal everyday stuff too intimate to share." He twisted his lips. "Not *we* like you and me but more like the collective we."

"You're right, there's a strange dichotomy between what a lot of guys consider mundane and what they hold sacrosanct." He trailed his fingers over Oliver's hip. "Finding someone where things line up is one of the biggest challenges in a relationship."

"That makes sense." Oliver nodded, looking thoughtful. "Where do you land on that?"

"Well, I'm not as casual about sex as say, a professional escort, but I'm not as conservative about it as my grandma who went to church every morning."

"Um, the range between those two extremes is so huge that when you stand at one end, you can't see the other."

"You're saying my explanation needs to be a little more explanatory?"

"A lot more."

"Fair enough." Jaime chuckled. "I slept with three different guys before I met Jack my senior year in college and then there was only him for ten years. After we ended it, I was too guilty to pursue anyone, so I had a long dry spell until, eventually, I decided to get out there again. I've been with five or six men since then, all of them I dated, though not always for long and not ever seriously." He reached for Oliver's hand and threaded their fingers together. "Until now."

"Oh." Oliver blinked. "So like ten people other than me."

"If you're going to turn everything involving two or more numbers into a math problem, I may make things interesting by throwing in a variable for you to solve."

"Ha, ha, ha."

"I'm not kidding. Think of all the fun I could have. Here, let's try it." Jaime wrapped his arm around Oliver and caressed his shoulder and bicep. "Last time I went to BevMo, I bought four bottles of white wine, three Malbecs, two whiskeys, a vodka, and 'X' cider bottles. If I handed the cashier sixteen bottles total, how many bottles of cider did I buy?"

"The better question is, when the cashier saw the size of your purchase did she 'A' ask you to join their frequent buyer program or 'B' hand you a brochure from AA?"

"It's a Walmart-sized liquor store with shopping carts. I have no doubt that the cashier spends her day ringing up orders larger than mine."

Oliver flipped onto his side and draped his arm over Jaime's hip, his hand landing on Jaime's butt. "We were having an important conversation about your views on sex and relationships and you changed the topic to the six cider bottles you bought."

Jaime threw his head back and laughed. "You can't stop yourself from calculating." He draped his leg over Oliver's and shifted closer, giving his dick much-wanted contact. "God, that's adorable."

"You may be the first person in the history of ever to describe a two-hundred ninety pound, six foot two grown man as adorable."

"Doubtful."

"Anyway," Oliver said, drawing out the word. "Back to what we were talking about."

"Remind me what I'm supposed to be explaining?" Jaime asked sincerely. "I gave you my list of exes."

"I know, I…" Oliver licked his lips, suddenly looking nervous. "I guess I…"

"Hey." Jaime cupped his cheek. "The reason I played along with the whole escort misunderstanding is because, when you thought I was him, you were comfortable being yourself and saying what you wanted, and I knew you wouldn't feel the same way with me if you realized I was just a regular guy who wanted to be with you. But—" He tilted Oliver's face up and met his gaze. "I'm still the same man you trusted with your secrets, still the same man who heard them and came back for more. Please don't be nervous. Not with me."

"That was different."

"No, it wasn't."

"It was, because before I told you things about *me*, this is…"

Jaime raised his eyebrows. "This is?"

"It's not about me."

Jaime rolled the conversation over in his head several times, but try as he might, he couldn't figure out what had tied Oliver up in knots. He thought over his options for a couple of minutes and decided the best way to know what Oliver wanted was for Oliver to tell him. He sat up, climbed over Oliver's groin, straddling him, and then lay down so they were connected from chest to thighs.

"Hey," he whispered. "Talk to me."

"I am talking."

Instead of arguing, Jaime gazed into Oliver's eyes and waited.

"I guess I just want to know what all of this means, like, tangibly."

"I'm usually pretty quick on the draw but apparently I'm having an off night so I'll need you to spell out what you're asking." He brushed his hand over Oliver's hair.

"You called me your boyfriend."

"Yes."

"To me, that means I don't see other people." Oliver's cheeks darkened. "Not that there's a line of guys knocking down my door or anything but I mean, like, theoretically, if there was a line or, uh, even one guy, I wouldn't—" He let out a deep breath. "Are you going to help me or are you just going to sit here and laugh?"

"Technically, I'm lying down, not sitting. And I'm not laughing either." He was curling his lips in to prevent them from forming a smile and his chest was vibrating but he wasn't actually laughing. "Technically."

"You're a mean boyfriend."

"Aww, I'm sorry, baby," Jaime drawled. "I'm not seeing anyone else either. That's what boyfriend means to me too, although I have to say I'm feeling a little old for that word." He kissed Oliver. "But in answer to what I think you're asking, I'm not one of those people who run in the other direction at the mention of commitment. I welcome it."

Oliver started chuckling.

"What?"

"Nothing." He shook his head. "I just got an image in my head."

"What image?" Jaime smiled. Oliver's happiness was infectious.

"You welcoming 'commitment.' Like you're all, come on in, Commitment. Have a seat. Can I get you some coffee, Commitment? How about a cheese Danish?"

"You are inordinately silly."

"I'm slaphappy."

"You're sexy."

"Be right back." Oliver started to wriggle.

"Where are you going?"

"I need to get my phone and change my relationship status on Facebook."

Jaime froze, partially on Oliver and partially on the mattress.

"And text my mom and my sister to tell them I have a boyfriend."

Jaime continued staring.

"What do you think the best way is to announce it on Twitter? That hundred forty character limit makes it so hard."

His jaw dropped.

"Do you mind if I take a picture of us to Snap? I'll make sure to keep it above the waist."

After hesitating for a couple of seconds, Jaime collapsed on Oliver and laughed. "You had me going!"

"That was fun." Oliver wrapped his arms and legs around Jaime. "I'm happy."

"Then it's worth the damage you caused by stopping my heart."

"I may have an idea to get it racing again," Oliver said, shyness creeping into his voice.

"Does your idea involve removing your boxers? Because if so, I'm in."

"That's funny because you being *in* is exactly what I had in mind."

The words were more certain than the tone, but uncertain or not, Oliver was flirting and playing in bed, things he wouldn't have done two months earlier. Jaime loved the proof of how comfortable previously reticent Oliver was with him.

"I appreciate how much you care about my cardiac health." He tilted his head to the side and pressed his lips to Oliver's in a soft kiss.

"I care about all of you," Oliver whispered into his mouth.

"Mmm." Jaime curled his hands around the sides of Oliver's neck, ran his thumbs along the edges of his jaw, and kissed him again.

Like he always did, Oliver seemed to relish the contact. He grasped at Jaime's shoulders and back, bucked his hips, and released a litany of whimpers and moans. Aroused by how fully and easily Oliver gave himself over to their passion, Jaime flicked his tongue over the seam of Oliver's lips and pressed his way into his mouth.

That apparently revved Oliver up further because he dug his fingernails into Jaime's back and feverishly sucked on his tongue.

Without pulling away from the kiss, Jaime reached his hand between them and grazed the bulge in Oliver's boxers.

"Jaime," Oliver gasped.

"You feel good." Jaime squeezed Oliver's erection. "Want to taste." He crouched above Oliver and slowly pushed his boxers down, exposing his hard cock. "Such a pretty dick." He scooched down so his face was level with Oliver's groin and licked a swath up his shaft before returning his focus to removing the underwear. "Have I told you that I love your legs?" He kissed and nibbled his way down Oliver's full thighs, pushed his boxers off, and then licked his way back up to Oliver's groin. "And your balls." He gently cupped the furry orbs and then lapped at them.

"Oh God." Oliver clutched at his shoulders.

Smiling, Jaime looked up at him, held onto the base of his shaft, and dropped his mouth over it.

His mouth falling open in a soundless gasp, Oliver arched his neck and spread his legs. Settling between the thick, hairy thighs, Jaime caressed Oliver's balls as he feasted on his dick, licking and sucking the hot flesh. He loved feeling the coarse hair contrasting with the soft skin, and he easily lost himself in the pleasure of his task, Oliver's flavor and scent flooding his brain.

"Jaime?" Oliver rasped. "You're so good at that, but…"

Mouth full of cock, Jaime raised his gaze.

"Will you top me?"

Instinctively, Jaime reached between his own legs, took hold of his cock, and stroked. "Yes," he answered, voice gravelly, his arousal rising as he thought about pushing his dick into tight heat. "Flip over for me, baby. Hands and knees."

Without hesitation, Oliver rolled onto his stomach and then rose to all fours.

Jaime ran his gaze over the new view and petted him appreciatively. "Give me a sec." He stretched across the bed to the nightstand and picked up the bottle of lube and a condom. Not wanting to stop once he was ready to go, he gave himself a few more strokes and then opened the wrapper and rolled the condom on.

Kneeling behind Oliver, he bent down, kissed his fleshy cheeks, and admiringly said, "Such a great ass." He planted a hand on each cheek and then squeezed and spread them, exposing Oliver's hole. "You ever been rimmed?"

Oliver looked over his shoulder, eyes wide, and shook his head.

"I get to be the first," he said, pleased.

"Jaime," Oliver gasped.

He held Oliver's cheeks open and licked the length of his channel, traveling down to his balls and back up and flicking his tongue over the sensitive skin to give Oliver as much sensation as possible. When Oliver's moans came closer together, Jaime zeroed his focus onto the circle of ridged skin and darted his tongue over it.

"Ah!" Oliver shouted, legs spreading wider, ass tilting higher.

Accepting the invitation, Jaime buried his face between the round cheeks and mouthed at Oliver's pucker, lips and tongue moving over the textured skin. He straightened his tongue, ran the tip in a circular pattern around Oliver's hole, and then held him still and pushed inside.

"Jaime!" Oliver screamed, entire body shaking. "Oh God. Oh God."

Wanting to give Oliver more pleasure, Jaime rubbed his thumbs around the hole as he tongued it. His own cock throbbed with need, but he forced himself to ignore it, focusing instead on Oliver. Through his moans and cries, Oliver told him how much he enjoyed Jaime's mouth on his ass, so Jaime continued licking and sucking. When he dipped the tips of his thumbs into the now wet hole, Oliver looked back over his shoulder and croaked, "Please."

"Anything," Jaime promised.

"Fuck me."

That was an easy promise to fulfill. Jaime clambered for the lube and then drizzled it onto his shaft and Oliver's channel. He pushed his thumbs inside and coated Oliver, and then he climbed up behind him, pressed the head of his cock against the hot, slick hole, and slid in.

"Ah," Oliver moaned. "Yes."

Slow, but steady, Jaime sank inside until his balls bounced against Oliver's. "Good?" he asked, voice sounding strained to his own ears.

"Uh-huh." Oliver's forehead was pressed to the mattress, his hands fisting the sheets. "I love you."

Despite the depth of his arousal, Jaime registered the words and his heart swelled. People often said things they didn't mean when passions ran high, but he didn't think that was true for Oliver. If anything, Oliver was more likely to share his feelings when his body's needs became so great that they pushed aside the worries in his mind. As for his own feelings, Jaime was amazed at how quickly he could recognize and revel in them when things felt right rather than forced.

"Love you too." He curled over Oliver and kissed his shoulder tenderly, taking a moment to relish the connection, and then he held on to Oliver's hips and began slamming into him. He varied his angle on every drive, wanting to find the one that would make Oliver sing, and when he heard a muffled whimper, he knew he'd hit his gland. "There?" he asked.

Not moving his body, Oliver bobbed his head, sweat-dampened hair flopping.

"Good." Jaime pulled out of the welcoming channel and punched back in, making sure to aim for Oliver's gland, and then he repeated the motion, staying on target with each pump. When his own end was near, he reached around Oliver's hip, took hold of his erection, and stroked.

"Ah, ah, ah." Oliver pushed back against Jaime harder and harder, shouts getting progressively louder.

"Come on, baby," Jaime encouraged, speeding up his tugs on Oliver's shaft. "Come on."

"Jaime!" Oliver cried out, and then his frantic motions halted and hot cream spilled over Jaime's fist.

"Yes!" Chasing his own orgasm, Jaime rammed into Oliver's tight hole until he reached the crest. "Yes!" he shouted again and ground his groin against Oliver's ass. "Yes," he moaned thickly as stream after stream of bliss shot from his cock. "Oliver." He clung to the body beneath him and trembled. "Yes."

Chapter 14

"WHAT WAS I thinking when I agreed to come here?" Oliver mumbled to himself as he looked out the windshield at the cars lined up along the curb.

"That it'd be nice to get out of the house and meet people?"

"Um, no. You must be confusing me with someone else because that's literally never something I think."

"You were thinking it's Halloween and it's fun to see people in costumes?"

"It's the twenty-ninth. Halloween is on Monday. And you didn't say people were dressing up. Is it going to be weird that I'm in normal clothes?"

"I'm not wearing a costume either. You'll be fine," Jaime assured him. "And when Halloween falls on a weekday, the Saturday before stands in for party purposes. That's a well-established rule."

"Who established it?"

"The party police," Jaime answered, deadpan.

"So now you're saying I don't know basic party laws? What if the party police arrest me? The safest thing for me to do is pass on the whole thing and maintain my criminal free history."

"Not showing up when we've already RSVP'd is a felony-level party crime. If you're worried about doing time, skipping out is definitely not the way to go." Jaime played along. Damn him for being so likeable.

"That's just it. I don't want to do party time," Oliver whined. "I don't know how I let you talk me into this."

"The sex addled your brain. Happens to the best of us."

"It was really great sex," Oliver agreed. A smile bloomed on his face at the memory until the sound of a car driving by knocked him back to the present. "You took advantage of my relaxed state to spring this on me." He crossed his arms over his chest and frowned.

"True and true." Jaime grinned. "Here's an idea. I'll pay you to come with me as my date. I happen to have…fifty dollars an hour times three hours times four weeks right in my wallet."

"You never spent the money I paid you for teaching me?"

"I never considered what I was doing a job, so I tucked the money aside, figuring we could decide what to do with it later." Jaime curled his hand around Oliver's nape. "Now it's later."

"Keep the money. Going in there is not worth seven hundred fifty bucks to me."

"You did the math wrong." Jaime's forehead creased. "That's not like you."

"I never do the math wrong. The first week was three hundred because I didn't have the discount from going to you directly."

"That's right. Whew." Jaime sighed dramatically. "You had me worried there for a sec. I thought the stress of this party had really gotten to you." He grinned. "Ready to go in or are we still in the middle of a freak-out?"

"*We* aren't in the middle of anything. *You're* perfectly calm."

"It looks that way on the outside because I have years of experience implementing the rule in those deodorant commercials. Inside I'm nervous too."

"What deodorant commercials?"

"Um, I think it was Dry Idea? Different people list things not to do in their field, and the last one is you never let them see you sweat, meaning that no matter how worried you are, you don't let it show."

"I haven't seen them, but I don't have a TV here, and back home when I watched network shows, I forwarded past the commercials."

Jaime groaned and closed his eyes.

"What?"

"You're making me feel old."

"You're not old."

"I'm old enough to have seen and remembered commercials that were made before you were born."

"Oh." Oliver blinked and thought that over. "That's funny." He smiled. "Here I was thinking you were talking about something new, and really, it's old." He chuckled. "My boy-friend's a geezer." The more he talked, the harder he laughed. "An incredibly good-looking, hot geezer, but still—"

"I think you're done being upset now," Jaime said, opening his door. "Let's go."

"Was it something I said?" Oliver asked, the words mangled through his laughter.

Jaime stepped out of the car.

"Jaime?" Oliver opened his door and hurried out. "Was it the 'hot' thing?" he asked, rushing after Jaime.

"Do guys your age prefer a different word?"

Not answering, Jaime walked down the sidewalk.

"How's handsome? You're a handsome geezer. Is that bet-ter?"

Keeping his pace, Jaime stepped to the side and made room for Oliver beside him.

"I'd like to point out that I also said, good-looking. That's not too flowery or too outlandish. Totally a baby bear's porridge compliment. It has to be acceptable to people from your generation."

"Are you intentionally highlighting our age difference by making nursery story references or is that just a fun coincidence?"

Oliver stumbled. "I totes didn't do that on purpose but I would have if I'd thought of it."

"Good to know." Jaime stopped walking and turned toward him. "We're here."

All of Oliver's humor vanished as he remembered where they were and why.

"Should I do the thing where I remind you that you want to meet people and make new friends?"

"No, I don't."

"You literally told me that was one of your goals."

"Just because I literally said it, doesn't mean I literally meant it." Oliver frantically shook his head. "It's like when someone says he's bored and wishes he had weekend plans but then he comes up with excuses when he's invited to do something."

"That's not a thing," Jaime said calmly.

"It's not?"

"No." Jaime stepped closer and slid his hand up Oliver's nape.

"I won't know anyone there," Oliver whispered.

"You'll know me."

He took a deep breath. "I'm worried about what your friends will think of me."

"You don't have to worry about that."

"Yes, I do. Look at you and then look at me."

"Are you referring to my old geezer status again?" Jaime asked, tone light.

"That was a joke. I'm being serious now. You're gorgeous and fun and smart and successful and the nicest guy I've ever met. You're pretty much perfect. And I'm—" Oliver pressed his lips tightly and sighed. "I'm a techy geek, which is redundant but true."

"Would it help if I reminded you that you're the perfect guy for me?" Jaime asked, voice soft. "I'm not sure how many people will be here tonight, but I probably won't know most of them, and the ones I do know will be guys I haven't spent time with since Jack and I separated."

Oliver managed to look past his own anxiety for long enough to remember Jaime saying he was nervous too.

"Your friends took his side in the breakup?"

"No, it wasn't contentious like that. There weren't sides. But even though we mutually agreed to part ways, it was harder on Jack, so he needed to lean on his support system. He wouldn't have been able to do that if I was there with everyone, acting like it was life as usual. Plus, I didn't want to make our friends feel like they had to alternate between us when they were making plans."

"So you made yourself scarce," Oliver summarized more than asked.

"Basically."

Gazing at the handsome face in front of him, Oliver knew Jaime's beauty ran much deeper than his grass-green eyes and strong jaw. Not being petty and vindictive to an ex was an accomplishment for most people, but Jaime treated Jack Storm with respect and compassion. If he treated an *ex*-boyfriend so generously, Oliver could only imagine how wonderful Jaime would be to a man he was actually seeing. If Oliver wanted to be that man, and he did, then he needed to show Jaime the same care and support he was certain he'd be receiving.

"You're sure it's okay to go to the party without costumes?" he asked, more as a step to get them into the house than as an actual question.

"My friend Kevin, the host, specifically said costumes were encouraged but *optional*. I choose to focus on the optional."

"You do have a knack for taking certain parts of what people say and running with them," Oliver pointed out, smiling. "Not that I can complain because your selective hearing is the reason I'm here."

Jaime had been right when he'd said the only reason Oliver had engaged with him was because he thought he'd been paying for Jaime's time. Without that misunderstanding, Oliver never would have had the confidence to speak to a man who looked like Jaime, let alone sleep with him. And if he had known Jaime was the person who'd written his favorite textbook and founded his company, Oliver probably wouldn't have been able to stay upright in his presence. Jaime's decision to play along with Oliver's misconception had resulted in him having everything he had fantasized about and more. Oliver had never been happier than he was at that moment and he recognized Jaime as the source of his joy.

"There's no place else I'd rather be than here at this party with you." Oliver straightened his shoulders, determined to stand by his boyfriend when he reclaimed something he had selflessly given up. "Let's go inside so you can introduce me to your friends."

OLIVER ESTIMATED THE attendance count at around six dozen total. Getting an actual tally was nearly impossible because people congregated in multiple rooms and many guests came late, explaining that they had attended other parties before that one, while others left early, presumably to do the same thing. It was also hard to distinguish between some of the men, many of whom looked alike. The ones in costumes were easier to tell apart, so Oliver had confidence that his number wasn't totally off.

"Did Thom tell you about his new house?" asked Kevin.

"No." Jaime smiled brightly at the black-haired man sitting across from them. "I think I remember you were looking in Capitol Hill."

"That was two houses ago. I sold the one in Capitol Hill last year when we bought the one we're in now."

"It's in Ballard," said the man sitting beside Thom. Oliver was eighty percent sure his name was Eric. "Total fixer-upper but we're almost done with it."

"Thank goodness." Thom leaned against his boyfriend. "I'm exhausted."

"Are you doing the work yourself?" Jaime asked, distractedly placing his hand on Oliver's thigh.

"What we can handle, yes."

"Tell Jaime about the bathroom," urged Kevin.

"Oh God." Thom groaned and closed his eyes. "I'm trying to block it out. You tell him, Eric."

"Okay. Where to start..." Eric mumbled. "In no particular order, there was floor to ceiling orange geometric print wallpaper, by which I mean, the wallpaper lined every inch of the walls and ceilings. In a small dose, the pattern wouldn't have been bad—"

"Small like a desktop picture frame," Thom interjected.

"Right. But covering the whole room, it was dizzying. Then, to make things worse, the tile was that old fifties Pepto Bismol pink color. Have you seen that?"

"Yes." Jaime nodded and laughed, his hand sliding over Oliver's leg in what seemed to be a subconscious show of affection.

"Okay, so you know it can be cute and vintage? Not in this bathroom. This tile was crumbling and moldy and like I said, the wallpaper was orange so there was also a clashing factor."

"Huge clashing factor," Thom agreed. "Tell him about the toilet."

"Right. The toilet, pedestal sink, and tub were all pea green."

"Cooked peas," Thom said. "Not the bright, clean green, but that muddy mushy color."

"Uh-huh." Eric nodded in agreement. "So we have the orange patterned wallpaper, the pink tiled shower surround, the pea-green fixtures, and then the coup de grace…" He paused dramatically.

"What?" Jaime asked.

"Carpet," Thom practically yelled. "They had *shag carpet* all around the toilet. We think it had started out pink but…" He shook his head disgustedly. "Tell him, Eric."

"It was more of a mustard color."

"Mustard! As in a mix of yellow and brown." Thom's face crinkled in disgust. "So pretty much the entire place was a biohazard."

The story was amusing, but listening to the way Thom and Eric told it in concert was what fascinated Oliver. They were completely in tune, filling in gaps and talking as one. Oliver had seen couples like that back home, older relatives or folks his mother knew from the library. But to witness that connection between two men, not much older than him, fanned a small flame of hope he usually forced himself to ignore.

"You have it all fixed up now?" Jaime asked, subtly squeezing Oliver's knee.

"Yes," Eric said. "We need to get the rest of the floors in the house installed and finish the kitchen and then we'll have people over."

"I'm so done with eating takeout." Thom hesitated and then lowered his voice. "You'll come, right, Jaime? You're done with the whole…" He waved his hand and cleared his throat. "You'll come to our housewarming party?"

"I wouldn't miss it." Jaime slid his hand from Oliver's knee back up to his thigh.

Thom beamed.

"In fact, I have the perfect idea for a housewarming present. What's the new color scheme in the bathroom? The wife of a colleague of mine makes custom painted toilet seats."

Oliver turned to the side and looked at Jaime, trying to figure out if he was kidding.

"You're joking," said Eric.

"Nope." Jaime shook his head. "She can do patterns too. Do you like checkers?"

"Jaime Snow, I carried your shit in and out of trucks in the rain and up three flights of stairs to that horrible little apartment you and Jack had in Belltown. Now that you have money, I expect an extravagant housewarming gift."

Jaime's chest shook with laughter. "Consider it done." He pushed his fingertips against Oliver's thigh and dragged them up and down, massaging him. "Oliver and I will get you something wonderful and expensive. Promise."

"Thank you," Thom said to Jaime and then he nodded at Oliver. "Thanks, Oliver."

Unsure how to react to being included in a gift for which he doubted Jaime expected him to pay, but more than that, how to react to being included in general, Oliver just nodded and softly said, "You're welcome."

"So, Oliver, you've heard our housing tale of woe. Where do you live?" Eric asked. "Or do you and Jaime live together?"

"You're in Laurelhurst, right?" Thom said, leaning forward excitedly. "Jack told us you have a gorgeous house on the lake."

"Yes." Jaime nodded. "If you want to get away from the construction mess or have a home-cooked meal, come on over. We'll make you dinner."

"That'd be great." Thom looked incredibly happy, too happy for the cause to be food, and Oliver suspected he considered Jaime a close friend, one he had been sad to lose and was thrilled to have back. "Wouldn't that be great, Eric?"

"It would." Eric wrapped his arm around Thom supportively.

"Should we schedule it now?" Thom asked hopefully.

"Absolutely." Jaime pulled out his phone and clicked through it. "Let's see. How about November twelfth. It's a Saturday." He glanced at Oliver. "Does that work for you, baby?"

Even though Oliver didn't know the men around him, didn't feel like he could contribute to the conversation, and hadn't spoken more than a few sentences all night, he felt included, maybe even important. At least to Jaime. "Sure," he said, knowing his own calendar showed blanks every weekend.

"That works for us too." Thom typed the appointment into his phone. "I'm excited to see your guys' house." His cheeks reddened and he glanced away. "I have to confess, I was sort of a stalker when Jack told us you bought it, so I've seen the seller's pictures online."

Feeling Jaime stiffen beside him, Oliver looked at him and saw a sad, guilty expression on his face.

"I'm sorry, Tommy," he rasped. "I didn't think about how shitty I was being to you guys. I just wanted—"

"He wanted to take care of me," said a deep, melodic voice. "Our Jaime always has been a knight in shining armor."

Thom and Eric looked up at the same time Jaime stood. Oliver twisted around to see Jack Storm standing behind him. He had seen pictures of his boss, watched videos, but he looked different in person. His eyes were still a beautiful denim blue, his short hair still a golden blond, and his body still strong and slender, but somehow the whole package appeared softer, more vulnerable.

"Jack," Jaime said warmly. He stepped around the couch and held his arms out.

Jack walked into his embrace and pecked his lips. "Glad you're here, Jaime."

They looked good together, both well built, classically handsome, polished. And there was no missing the history and affection between them. They fit and Oliver's stomach tightened uncomfortably at the sight. Why would Jaime be with him when he could have Jack Storm?

Several long seconds passed before Jack stepped away from Jaime and looked over at the rest of the men gathered around. "Sorry I'm late, Kevin." He walked up to Kevin and hugged him. "I had to make a showing at a few other parties and I saved the best for last." He raised his chin in the direction of the sofa across from him. "Eric, Thom. Love the costumes."

Eric wore a tight red T-shirt and red hat while Thom wore a matching green shirt and green hat. When Oliver had realized they were dressed as Mario and Luigi, his worry about not fitting in had eased. He was around fellow gamers, even if the game was old-school Nintendo.

"And this must be the wonderful Oliver Barnaby Jaime can't stop talking about." Jack approached him, and Oliver instinctively rose to his feet. "I'm so happy to finally meet you, Oliver," Jack said, voice sincere. "I owe you a thank-you for helping Jaime take care of Rex while I was out of town. I know it was very last minute." He held his hand out to Oliver.

Until that moment, Oliver hadn't put two and two together and realized the Jack who owned the gorgeous home in Millionaire's Row was the same Jack who Jaime had dated for ten years, not to mention the same Jack who ran his company.

"It wasn't a problem." After wiping his palm on his pant leg, Oliver took Jack's hand, hoping Jack wouldn't notice his trembling. "Your dog is sweet and your home is beautiful."

"Sweet?" Jack looked at him disbelievingly. "Either you have the same magical touch as Jaime when it comes to animals, or you're being polite."

Jaime walked up and stood beside Oliver. "Rex liked him. I told you our boy's an angel."

Jack huffed. "A dozen dog sitters, veterinary technicians, and groomers would disagree with you on that point, but I'm glad he took a shine to Oliver."

Maybe not a shine, but the dog had approached him a few times for scratches and pets, and he certainly hadn't seemed upset with his presence. "He's a great dog," Oliver said.

"That he is," Jack agreed. He tilted his head toward the edge of the sofa where Jaime and Oliver had been sitting. "Is that spot taken?"

"Uh, no." The couch wasn't huge but it could fit three men, as long as they didn't mind tight quarters. Oliver wasn't particularly comfortable sitting so close to a man he didn't know and simultaneously admired and resented, but the alternative was sitting on the other edge of the couch and giving Jaime the middle seat, which would put him shoulder to shoulder and hip to hip with his ex. Not going to happen. Oliver plopped down in the center of the sofa.

"I'll get us more drinks." Jaime picked up his empty beer bottle and Oliver's empty cup. "Jack, you want a scotch and soda?"

"Please." Jack sat down beside Oliver. "Thank you."

With an acknowledging nod at Jack and a squeeze of Oliver's shoulder, Jaime walked away. It wasn't the first time Oliver had been without him at the party—Jaime had wandered off to get them snacks and drinks throughout the night, and he had been pulled away more than a few times by men who wanted a few minutes of privacy with their old friend—but this time, Oliver was sitting beside the dashingly handsome, uber successful, smoothly confident man who had shared nearly half of his new boyfriend's life. If Jack Storm couldn't hold on to Jaime, what chance did Oliver have?

"How's work?" Thom asked Jack.

"Good." Jack leaned forward, forearms braced on his knees. "Insanely busy, but good. How about you?"

"Boring. I pretty much play *Sims* all day."

Jack snorted and then looked at Oliver. "Has Thom already told you what he does?"

Oliver shook his head.

"He works for the Federal Public Defender's Office death

penalty appeals unit. He barely has time for coffee, let alone web surfing."

"I should start," Thom said. "Maybe in the virtual world, I'd actually be able to help somebody."

Eric looked at him sympathetically. "You do everything you can. What happened before you met them is out of your control."

"Eric's right, Tommy. You do admirable work."

Thom smiled appreciatively, and Oliver realized that on top of all his other attributes, Jack Storm was nice. Honestly, how could he compete?

"I know what you're thinking, and you don't have anything to worry about," Jack said, voice so quiet Oliver could barely make out the words.

He turned toward him and blinked, trying to figure out if Jack had been talking to him or mumbling to himself.

"You're more his type than I ever was."

Oliver's disbelief must have shown on his face because Jack's lips rose in a sad smile and he leaned closer.

"Just because people look good together on paper, doesn't mean they're right for each other." Jack's expression turned thoughtful. "As much as we might wish otherwise, real life isn't a game, and if we use our cheat codes to manipulate someone into doing something he doesn't want, everybody loses."

"Beverage delivery," Jaime said as he approached, his large hands wrapped around a bottle and two cups. He set them all down on the end table and then began distributing them. "Jack, here's your scotch." He handed Jack a cup. "Here you go, baby." He gave Oliver his drink and then sat down beside him, palm immediately resting on Oliver's knee. "What'd I miss?"

Chapter 15

"I'M GLAD YOU decided to talk to Jack about the issue with the female characters."

Fingers halting over the shirt button he was opening, Oliver arched his eyebrows incredulously and said, "*Decided?* You told me to tell him."

"I think it's important, so I suggested it, but I'm glad you felt comfortable enough with him to do it." Jaime pushed his dark jeans to his ankles and then neatly hung them.

"He was sitting right next to us and you literally said, 'Oliver, tell Jack what you were saying about the issue with the women in Snow Storm's games.' What was my other option?"

"You could have run away screaming." Jaime yanked his shirt over his head. "Faked a seizure." He tossed the shirt in the laundry hamper. "Spilled a drink all over me and then insisted on helping me off with my clothes and seduced me."

Shirt halfway off his shoulders, Oliver froze. "That last one was an option?"

Jaime chuckled. "Seriously though. He saw your point and appreciated that you brought it to his attention. Now that he's aware of it, he'll work on making changes. Jack's a doer."

"It's an uphill battle," Oliver said, stripping off the rest of his clothes. "Seems like it shouldn't be a big deal to fix something so easy, but most of the designers don't see the issue and a few of them are like adamantly opposed to making changes." He shook his head. "They started calling me a Social Justice Warrior because I'm pushing to have a black ops soldier dress like a black ops soldier instead of a Playboy Bunny."

"Social Justice Warrior?" Jaime asked as they walked into the bedroom.

"It's not a compliment."

"Didn't figure it was." Jaime climbed into bed and watched Oliver do the same on the other side. After having Oliver in his house for one night, Jaime already wanted it to be *Oliver's side*. "Internal operations are Jack's bailiwick, but I've been looking into this, and I think we can help outside of our four walls by sponsoring organizations and scholarships for girls who code. Apparently there are good programs out there working to get more girls interested in our industry."

"That's a great idea." His chest and groin on display, Oliver fluffed his pillow and adjusted his blanket while Jaime watched, enjoying the show. "I didn't notice it until I started talking about it with Tamra, but there really aren't enough women at Snow Storm or, according to her, other game companies. Changing those ratios in our design team would go a long way toward having better representations in our characters."

"Knowing Jack, he'll form an advisory committee to look into this. If you tell him you want to work on it, he'll include you."

Oliver stilled and his eyes widened. "No."

"Why not?" Jaime asked, surprised at that reaction.

"Because, Jaime—" Oliver sighed and then finally lay down. "A committee put together by the CEO is a big deal. Everyone will want to be on it. I can't get special treatment just because I'm dating the boss."

"I'm not your boss." Jaime shook his head. "Everything I do

involves outside services."

"You own half the company and you have a direct line to the man in the huge corner office on the top floor." Oliver crossed his arms over his chest.

"There are at least a handful of people between you and Jack on the org chart. You don't report to him." Even as he said the words, Jaime knew they were ridiculous. Direct report or not, Oliver's relationship with him meant people would be more respectful and deferential to him. It gave him an edge. "But yes, you will get special treatment. So what?"

"That's not right." Oliver fidgeted. "It's like sleeping my way to the top." He frowned. "Which, by the way, is not a method of success I ever saw as an option for me, so yay, but no."

"You're not sleeping your way to the top."

"You just said I'll get special treatment."

"Not because you're sleeping with me. Hell, if I'd known where you worked when I met you, I never would have—" Jaime stopped short and thought about what he was about to say. If he had known the handsome, sweet, shy guy clutching his textbook at the bar was Snow Storm's newest employee, would he have turned around and walked in the opposite direction? No. "That's not true." He shook his head. "I would have approached you even if I had known. But it wouldn't have been to get you into bed. It would have been to get to know you better and hopefully end up where we are now." He curled his palm around Oliver's cheek. "Half of business is connections. Who you know matters. It may not be fair, but it's life. You're not trading sex for favors. The guy who owns half your company is in love with you. If that comes with advantages at the office, well—" Jaime shrugged. "Use your power for good not evil."

"You're in love with me?" Oliver whispered.

"Yes." Jaime scooted closer, wrapped his arms around Oliver, and pressed their foreheads together. "I love you, Oliver."

"Last night when we were… But I wasn't sure if you meant it or even realized you said it because heat of the moment and all that. I didn't want to push you so I didn't mention it."

"I knew exactly what I was saying and I absolutely meant it." Jaime brushed his lips over Oliver's. "This is your first real relationship, you're in a new job in a new city, and I'm not who you thought I was. That's a lot of change in a short time and I don't want to overwhelm you, so I'm trying to let you set the pace, but you don't need to worry about pushing me. If it were up to me, this thing would get dialed up to ten yesterday."

"I want that too, and I'm not overwhelmed, but I think I need a little time to process everything."

"Not a problem." Jaime instinctively tightened his hold on Oliver, hoping the processing could wait until Monday morning so it wouldn't disrupt their time together. Thankfully, Oliver melted into his embrace rather than pulling away.

"Maybe Tamra will want to be on Jack's advisory committee."

"Your friend who brought all this to your attention?"

"Yes." Oliver nodded. "She's been at Snow Storm a lot longer than I have, and she's worked at other game companies. Plus, she's a woman. If Jack wants someone with insight into this issue, Tamra's a good choice."

"Sounds like it. I'll mention her name to Jack. Thanks for the suggestion."

"I'm using my power for good." Oliver smiled.

"Nicely done." Jaime slid his fingers through Oliver's soft brown hair. "What did you think of the party tonight? Was it as horrible as you thought it would be?"

"I didn't think it'd be horrible!"

Jaime didn't say anything.

"Okay, fine, I wasn't excited about going." Oliver laid his head on Jaime's chest. "Your friends were really nice and interesting." He ran his fingers through Jaime's chest hair. "It wasn't horrible."

"They liked you."

"I was too quiet."

Jaime had never been drawn to men who had to fill every silence with noise and who needed all eyes on them. Eventually, Oliver would be more engaged in conversations with other people, but he couldn't imagine him ever clamoring to be the center of attention, which was perfect. "You'll feel more comfortable the more time you spend with them."

Oliver walked his fingertips down Jaime's stomach, tracing over the lines of his muscles. "Your friends missed you," he said softly.

"I missed them too. More than I realized." He had met wonderful people in the years since he and Jack had broken up, but they couldn't take the place of the friends he'd had when he was young and starting out.

"And Jack?" Oliver asked, voice cracking.

"What about Jack?" Jaime furrowed his brow, trying to figure out what was worrying Oliver.

"He seems like a good guy. You two looked really close. You own a business together."

Ah, that was it. "He is. We are. We do." Jaime met Oliver's gaze. "But there isn't and never has been any chemistry between us. I tried to talk myself into it for years, but eventually, I learned that you can't convince yourself to be attracted to someone. You don't need to be jealous of Jack. He isn't a threat to us."

"I know. That's not why I was asking."

"It isn't?"

"No." Oliver shook his head. "I get that you're not interested in him."

"Then what's upsetting you?"

"I guess I'm wondering." Oliver let out a deep breath. "If a guy like that isn't good enough to keep your attention, what chance do I have?"

Jaime cringed. "It's not a matter of good enough. Whoever Jack ends up with is going to be beyond lucky. But he and I weren't a good match. There weren't butterfly stomachs or racing hearts or distracted minds when I was with him." Jaime never aired his and Jack's dirty laundry, but he needed Oliver to understand that what he could see blooming between them, what they already shared after less than two months, wasn't the same as his previous relationship. "Going to bed with him was an obligation. It got to the point where I dreaded it." Jaime gulped, remembering the stress of those years. "He didn't deserve to live like that."

"Neither did you."

"It wasn't his fault. He didn't do anything wrong. I just… The chemistry wasn't there. He's like a brother to me."

After a minute of silence, Oliver asked, "At the beginning with him, was it different?" He reached for Jaime's hand. "I'm not trying to be nosy and I know there aren't guarantees in life but I feel like I'm at the edge of a sharp cliff and I need to know if I should strap into a parachute before I jump."

"Are you asking if I run hot at first and then get bored?" Jaime asked, threading his fingers with Oliver's.

"Something like that, yeah."

"No, I don't," Jaime answered. "Jack and I never had a love

affair. We were friends, good friends. But that's all. It wasn't a matter of passion running dry. Some men I've dated after him did it for me physically, but we didn't have anything in common outside of the bedroom. I need both." He moved his thumb over Oliver's palm. "With you, I can have an interesting conversation or spend a quiet night in and I'm happy and engaged, and you already know how strongly my body reacts to you." He drove his groin forward, rubbing his erection against Oliver's leg. "You're the whole picture."

Firm, warm fingers wrapped around Jaime's dick. "I feel the same way about you."

Eyes drooping in reaction to Oliver's intimate touch, Jaime groaned. "You make me so hard," he rasped and spread his legs, giving Oliver more room. "It's so good."

"I'm glad it's not just me feeling this way." Oliver slid his fist up and down Jaime's shaft.

"Absolutely not." Jaime took hold of Oliver's dick and started stroking. "This is completely mutual." With his free hand, he tweaked Oliver's nipple.

"Ungh." Oliver bucked, pushing his cock through Jaime's fist. "I'm already close."

The speed with which he could bring Oliver to the edge was flattering.

"Go for it," he said, his voice a rough croak. Slamming his lips against Oliver's, Jaime kissed him hard while he jerked his dick and played with his nipples. "Come all over me."

A few more pulls and Oliver was clutching both his biceps, screaming into his mouth, and shooting over his hand. "God." Oliver's chest heaved. "So good."

Good and insanely arousing. Seeing Oliver lost in pleasure brought Jaime's orgasm to the surface. He wrapped his cum-slick hand around his own dick and tugged. "Yes," he hissed. "Going to."

Heated brown eyes watched him, clearly enjoying the show.

"This is because of you," Jaime confessed. "You do this to me." He stroked faster. "Make me feel so much." Early seed seeped from his slit. "Make me feel so good."

"Jaime," Oliver whispered his name reverently. "You're so beautiful."

"So are you, baby." Jaime's eyes roamed over the gorgeous body beside him, thick and full, masculine. "So are you." He rolled Oliver onto his back, climbed on top of him, and sucked on his neck as his hand flew over his own dick. "Oliver. Oliver. Oliver."

Hands landed on his ass, pulling him forward encouragingly.

"Oliver!" he shouted joyfully as his dick pulsed out thick, white cream. "Love you." He kissed his way up Oliver's jaw and over to his ear as he caught his breath. "Love you so much," he whispered. "Thank you for coming with me tonight." He had been nervous about walking back into a life he had abandoned years earlier and having Oliver by his side had given him support and strength.

"Thank you for including me." Oliver's hands roamed over Jaime's back, exploring and caressing. "You made me feel like an important part of your life."

"You are." He hugged Oliver tightly. "More important than you can imagine."

Chapter 16

"WHY NOT?" TAMRA demanded.

"Because it's a one-bedroom," Oliver said for the third time in the last five minutes. He rolled down the paper on his turkey sub and took a bite.

"And Craig is one person. It's perfect."

"I'm one person too," Oliver said through his mouthful of food. He picked up his cup and sucked down some pop. "One plus one equals two, and I'm not interested in sleeping with your brother."

"Who said anything about you sleeping with my brother?"

"You did when you started harassing me about letting him move into my apartment." Oliver reached into the foil bag beside him and snagged two chips.

"Quit playing dumb, Oliver. We both know you better than that."

He pushed away the last of his sandwich and sighed. "So what am I supposed to do? Just tell Jaime I'm moving into his house? 'Hi. How was your day? We've been together six months now so I've decided it's time for me to move in and Tamra's brother is going to sublet my place. Do you mind clearing out some room in your closet for me?'"

Not that Jaime would need to do a thing to make space for him. The man's closet was huge and had more than enough empty shelves for the rest of Oliver's belongings. Many of his clothes already hung there.

"Are you seriously trying to get me to believe that he hasn't ever asked you to live with him?" Tamra raised her eyebrows and shook her head. "Nuh-huh. I'm not buying it."

"He hasn't."

Her eyebrows went higher.

"He hasn't!" Oliver said emphatically.

"I should have gotten a twelve inch." Tamra picked at a crumb on her empty wrapper. "I always tell myself the six inch will be enough and then I'm not satisfied."

"I feel like I ought to be making a crude joke here," Oliver said, pushing his chips toward her.

"Not everything is about a dick," she said drolly.

"Sorry." Oliver's neck warmed.

"You're forgiven on one condition."

Knowing what that condition would be, he cut her off at the pass. "Your brother can find a different apartment."

"The real estate market sucks, your rent is really reasonable, and your place is walking distance to the job Craig got." She raised a finger with each point. "Come on, Oliver, when was the last time you even slept there?"

"A few days ago." But only because he made a point of going to his own house on the nights Jaime had late meetings.

Her unimpressed gaze locked on him, she picked up the bag, leaned back in her chair, and began eating the chips.

Oliver tried to ignore her, but the silent stare eventually got to him. "Things are really good between us." More than good, actually. From the first night, he had felt safe with Jaime and the sex had always been outstanding, but after Halloween weekend, when Jaime had confessed who he really was, they'd continued growing closer, and now Oliver couldn't imagine being without him. "I don't want to ruin it."

"Explain to me why you think moving into your boyfriend's house, a house in which you already spend nearly all of your free time, is going to ruin your good relationship?"

Needing a distraction, Oliver crumpled up his trash. "I guess it won't."

"So what's the issue?"

"I don't know." Oliver's favorite part of the day was waking up in Jaime's arms or falling asleep in them. He loved curling up with him on the couch and watching old movies. They shared dinner most nights and spent their weekends together. Oliver even enjoyed hanging out with Jaime's friends, some of whom he now considered his own friends. "I guess I feel like it's his house so I should wait for him to ask me to live there."

"I've seen the way that man looks at you not to mention the way he's always touching you. I don't believe he's never broached the topic of you moving in with him."

"I guess he has in a way." He had Jaime's door code, one of his garage door openers, and an open invitation to come over whether Jaime was home or not. He had been Jaime's plus one at dozens of events, with Jaime always taking the time to introduce him and include him in conversations in a way that implied he was important. Jaime checked with him before making plans, confirming if he was available. He had even met Jaime's parents when they'd been in town for a visit. Basically, Jaime had integrated Oliver into every aspect of his life and done everything possible to show Oliver he was valued. "I'm pretty sure he's waiting for me to be ready," Oliver admitted. And Jaime was selfless enough to wait as long as Oliver needed without harassing him or complaining. The more Oliver thought about it, the more he realized he didn't need the safety net of his apartment, not when it came to Jaime. "When's your brother moving here?"

"Middle of the month."

Sometimes, when Oliver woke up before Jaime, he gazed at the handsome face on the pillow beside him and pinched himself to make sure he wasn't trapped in the best dream of his life.

"I can be out of my place by then." Out of his lonely apartment and living with the most wonderful man he had ever met. Now that he'd made the decision to tell Jaime he wanted to move in with him, Oliver wondered what had taken him so long.

Tamra beamed. "I'll tell Craig."

OLIVER DIDN'T FANCY himself a great cook, but he had a few solid recipes in his repertoire and he prepared one of them for what he hoped would be a memorable meal. This would be an evening he and Jaime would look back on when they thought about the milestones in their relationship and he wanted everything to be perfect.

After adding another dash of salt and pepper to his grandmother's chicken cacciatore, he put the lid on the skillet and left it simmering on the stove while he set the table. Fifteen minutes later, the chicken was done, the asparagus was blanched, and the loaf of French bread he had picked up at the grocery store was sliced. Trying to keep himself occupied so he wouldn't call Jaime to ask if he was almost home, Oliver fiddled with the flowers he had arranged in one of Jaime's crystal vases. Just as he was about to break down and send Jaime a text, the dogs started barking and running for the door.

"Oh, thank God," Oliver muttered.

He turned off the burner, which he had set to low, got the butter out of the fridge, and poured cold water into their glasses. After taking a last appraising look around the kitchen and satisfying himself that everything looked perfect, or at least as good as he could make it, he wiped his hands on a towel and then walked in the direction of Jaime's voice.

"Yes, you're a good girl. Oliver and I will take you for a walk later."

He turned the corner and found Jaime squatting in the hall-way, petting Kiki and Lulu. The familiar sight calmed his fraying nerves.

"Hi. How was your day?"

At the sound of his voice, Jaime looked up and smiled tired-ly. "Getting better by the minute."

"You want to talk about it?" Oliver asked, recognizing the answer to mean Jaime'd had a rough day.

"We were supposed to finalize a deal with a growing retail chain, but their head buyer quit unexpectedly and the new guy they put on the account couldn't focus on the negotiations because he was busy making what I assume were supposed to be jokes and then laughing at them. Seven people in the room and he was the only one who thought he was funny." Jaime stood, and the dogs ran off, yipping happily at each other. "It's not interesting. Just work." He stepped over to Oliver, wrapped his arm around Oliver's waist, cupped his cheek, and leaned in for a kiss. "I'm glad to be home."

Instinctively, Oliver leaned into Jaime and parted his lips.

"Mmm." Jaime slid his tongue over Oliver's lower lip and then tugged that lip between both of his. "Been looking forward to this all day."

"Me too." Oliver wound his arms around Jaime's neck, relishing the press of Jaime's hard body against his.

Pulling him closer, Jaime slipped his fingers through Oliver's hair and pressed their mouths together again. This time he pushed his tongue past Oliver's lips, taking the kiss deeper.

At six two and nearly three hundred pounds, Oliver was bigger than most people, but Jaime was taller and significantly more muscular, so when Oliver melted against him, Jaime had no trouble supporting his weight.

"Come here, baby." His left hand lowering to Oliver's butt and his right tangling in his hair, Jaime pulled Oliver closer and rocked his hips, grinding against him. "You smell good." Jaime inhaled deeply. "Like that oatmeal soap. Did you already shower?"

"Uh-huh." He had showered, spent more time than was reasonable on his hair, and brushed his teeth twice.

"Wish I'd been here to join you," Jaime mumbled into his mouth and then kissed him again.

"We can take another shower after dinner," Oliver offered.

"Good idea. Do you mind if we order in? I'm too beat to go out."

Remembering what he had planned for the night, Oliver glanced away nervously. "Actually, I cooked."

"You did?" Jaime said, sounding pleased. "That's even better. What'd you—" His phone rang, stopping him mid-sentence. "That's Jack. I sent him a text after that meeting to let him know the timeline on that deal has to change. He probably wants more details." He took his phone from his pocket, held it up, and looked at Oliver questioningly. "It'll only take a couple of minutes."

When they were together, Jaime focused on Oliver, not his phone, but being as busy as he was, meant he occasionally got calls and texts he couldn't ignore. Even then, he checked with Oliver before answering them. It was one of the many ways Jaime made him feel valued and respected.

"Go ahead," Oliver said. "I'll get dinner plated."

Answering the phone as they began walking toward the kitchen, Jaime said, "Hey, Jack. Did you see my text about—" Face suddenly awash in concern, Jaime came to a sudden stop. "Jack? Are you okay? What's going on?"

Although bits and pieces of Jack's voice drifted over, Oliver couldn't make out any words. He looked at Jaime questioningly.

"We'll be right over," Jaime rasped. "We're getting in the car now." He ended the call and looked at Oliver, his expression devastated. "Jack's mother died."

IN THE SIX months Oliver had been with Jaime, he had spent a decent amount of time with Jack Storm. The private Jack wasn't as polished and formal as the Snow Storm CEO, but in his personal time as well as his professional time, Jack was always calm, put-together, and fairly unemotional. So walking into Jack's house to find him crumpled on the couch, eyes red and swollen, took Oliver by surprise.

"Jack," Jaime said, voice breaking, as he rushed into the room.

"She's gone." Jack raised sad eyes toward Jaime.

"I know." Jaime sat beside Jack, wrapped his muscled arms around him, and pulled his head against his chest. "I know."

Oliver stood hesitantly in the doorway, watching Jack cling to Jaime, his body trembling.

As he was with most people, Oliver had been nervous and uncomfortable around Jack at first. Those natural tendencies were exacerbated because of who Jack was—the man who ran his company, the man who still held a valued position in Jaime's life, the man everyone seemed to like. But that last attribute had worked its magic on Oliver too, and he had let his guard down around Jack sooner than he would have expected of himself. And although he had occasionally noticed Jack looking at him and Jaime with a wistful expression, Jack had always been nice and welcoming to Oliver.

Not wanting to intrude on what was clearly a personal moment, Oliver quietly left the room. His first stop was the bathroom, where he found a box of tissues under the cabinet. Next, he stopped in the kitchen and got a bottle of water from the fridge. After standing around for another couple of minutes, he headed back to the living room, hoping he had given Jack the time he needed alone with Jaime.

"Remember that night we went to dinner at her favorite restaurant, but she didn't know the address or the name?" Jaime was saying as Oliver stepped into the room.

"Oh God." Jack laughed through his tears. "That was hilarious." He must have sensed movement from the corner of his eye because he looked up and met Oliver's gaze. "Oliver, hi." He sniffled, disentangled himself from Jaime and waved Oliver over. "You can come in."

"I'm sorry for your loss," Oliver said as he shuffled toward them, feeling awkward. "I, uh, thought you might need some tissues." He held the box out to Jack. "And water." He threw his other hand forward.

"Thank you." Jack pulled a few tissues out, wiped his nose, and then gulped down the water.

"Sit with us, baby." Jaime curled his hand around Oliver's thigh and patted the empty cushion beside him.

"Are you sure? I can give you priva—"

"Jaime was just reminding me of a funny story about my mom." Jack put the cap on the bottle and tightened it. "How long ago was that, Jaime?"

"Forever. At least ten years, right? Maybe fifteen?"

Jaime gently tugged on Oliver's leg, so he sat down, still holding the box of tissues.

"Thirteen I think." Jack wiped the back of his hand across his eye. "Because Lindy was still a baby."

"That's right," Jaime agreed. "We were visiting Jack's parents for his mom's birthday, and so were his sister and her family. Lizbeth"—Jaime looked at Oliver—"Jack's mother, had been going on and on about her favorite new restaurant so we decided to go there for dinner. We couldn't all fit in one car so Lizbeth, Carol—"

"My sister," Jack explained.

"And the three kids went in one car and Jack's dad, his brother-in-law, and the two of us went in another. She didn't remember the address of the restaurant."

"Or the name," Jack said.

"Or the name," Jaime agreed. "So we were following her. It was fine at first and then all of a sudden, she went full Bourne, weaving around traffic, running red lights."

"My dad tried to keep up, Jaime and I grabbed onto the doors so we wouldn't be jostled around too much in the backseat, and my brother-in-law started cussing up a storm."

Jaime rolled his eyes at the mention of Jack's brother-in-law. "We found the place eventually," he said.

"Turns out the baby had started crying and the other two kids were fighting so my mom was trying to get them there as fast as possible."

"NASCAR style."

Jack's eyes were still red-rimmed, his nose still stuffed, but now he was chuckling. "I don't think my dad's hands stopped shaking that whole meal." He sighed and leaned his head against the back of the couch. "He's going to be a mess without her."

Jaime nodded quietly.

"My flight's in three hours." Jack set the water bottle beside him and wiped his palms on his pants. "I better pack."

"We'll get Kiki and Lulu and come back here to stay with Rex," Jaime said.

"Thanks." Jack stood, and with a deep sigh, he walked out of the room, looking exhausted.

"Jaime," Oliver said.

"Hmm?" Jaime caressed his thigh.

"Do you think Jack would want you to go with him?"

Jaime's eyes widened. "I don't know. I haven't been home with him since before we broke up."

Which made perfect sense, in normal circumstances. "He seems like he could use the support."

"You're right." Jaime nodded.

"I can stay here with the dogs."

Jaime turned to Oliver and cupped both his cheeks. "You're wonderful." He brushed their noses together and then kissed Oliver. "I love you."

"I love you too." Oliver clutched Jaime's waist, leaned into him, and took one kiss after another, needing the connection before Jaime left town. "We better go home so you can pack."

"Yeah." Jaime bit Oliver's lower lip, licked it, and then pulled away. "I'll go tell Jack what's going on and get his flight info so I can try to get on his same flight."

Oliver nodded and watched Jaime's muscular butt as he

walked away. When he reached the doorway, he stopped and looked at Oliver over his shoulder. "Thank you."

"Nothing to thank me for."

"I have everything to thank you for." Jaime's expression was soft and affectionate. "I'll make sure to do it properly when I get home."

Chapter 17

TEN DAYS WAS too long for Jaime to be away from his dogs, his work, and most importantly, it was too long for him to be apart from Oliver. But Oliver had been right to suggest that he accompany Jack on his trip. In the nearly two decades they had known each other, Jaime had never seen his friend so fragile and vulnerable. His being there to navigate family drama, consult about hard decisions, and offer a shoulder to cry on had helped Jack, so Jaime was glad he had gone. He was also glad to be home.

His first phone call when the airplane wheels hit the ground was to Oliver.

"Hey, are you back?"

"Just landed."

"I bet you're exhausted. I should be able to leave work at a decent hour today. Want me to pick up dinner on my way home?"

"I am tired." Jaime dragged his fingers through his hair. "But don't bother stopping for dinner. I'll have something delivered. That way I can see you as soon as possible."

"Okay." Oliver sounded pleased. "I took Kiki and Lulu to your house this morning before I went into the office. I think Rex was relieved to see them go."

"I bet he was." Jaime chuckled. The seatbelt sign dinged and people started rising from their seats. "Thanks for taking care of everything, baby."

"It wasn't a problem. I hope Jack's okay."

Jaime glanced at Jack, who was getting their bags down from the overhead bins. "He will be."

Apparently realizing they were talking about him, Jack looked down. "Thank him for me."

"Jack says thanks too."

As usual, Oliver had trouble accepting gratitude. His generosity was as endearing as his shyness.

"I, uh, I'll see you tonight," Oliver said.

"See you tonight. I love you."

"Me too." Oliver's voice was lower, and Jaime could imagine him at his desk, blushing even though nobody else could hear his side of the call. "Bye."

He stood and put the phone in his pocket.

"Here you go." Jack handed him his bag and they walked off the plane.

"Are you going to ask him tonight or are you waiting for the weekend?"

"I was going to wait so I could plan something memorable or make reservations somewhere romantic but..."

"You're too excited to hold off that long?" Jack smiled in understanding.

Jaime shrugged. "It'll be a miracle if he can get one foot in the door before I'm on one knee."

"He's a great guy, Jaime." Jack bumped their shoulders together. "And he's perfect for you."

There was no resentment in Jack's voice, no bitterness, and Jaime knew that he hadn't lost his friend when he finally found someone he could love.

"He is." Jaime threw his free arm around Jack's shoulders. "Hopefully he'll say yes."

"Hopefully?" Jack arched his eyebrows. "Nobody can resist

the James Snow charm." He shook his head. "I'm dusting off my tux when I get home because this thing's in the bag."

As it turned out, Jaime managed to keep himself in check through Oliver's arrival home, dinner, and their nightly walk with the dogs. He considered waiting longer so he could plan something special but then he looked at Oliver curled up against him on the couch, socked feet tucked under his thighs, hair mussed, and he knew the *something special* was what they had between them.

"Where are you going?" Oliver asked when he got up.

Rather than answering with words, Jaime stepped in front of him and then lowered himself to one knee.

"Jaime?" Oliver's voice cracked.

He reached for Oliver's hands, held both of them between his own, and met his hopeful gaze. "My whole life, I've wanted you. When I was a kid, just figuring out who I was and realizing I wasn't interested in women, you were the guy I daydreamed about. When I was in college and starting to date, you were the man I kept hoping to find. When my business took off and I was surrounded by amazing friends, living a life everyone thought was perfect, you were what I was missing. And when I wandered through this house alone, night after night, year after year, you were the person I imagined living here beside me." Jaime licked his lips and swallowed down the thickness in his throat. "And then I met you and you exceeded every hope, every dream, and every fantasy." He raised Oliver's hands to his mouth and kissed the back of each one. "Marry me, Oliver," he rasped. "Please marry me."

Eyes wet and lips pressed together, Oliver bobbed his head. "Yes." He blinked rapidly, slid off the couch, and threw his arms around Jaime's shoulders. "Yes."

Heart full to bursting yet light as air, Jaime hugged Oliver tightly. "Love you."

"I love you too." Oliver sniffled and then laughed. "And this is really good timing."

"Why's that?" Jaime's hands roamed over Oliver's back, enjoying his warm, yielding body.

"Tamra's brother is moving to Seattle this weekend." Oliver pulled his face away from Jaime's shoulder, met his gaze, and grinned. "Right before you left town, I told him he could have my place, so I had to move out. I've been driving around with everything I own stuffed in the back of my car, hoping you wouldn't mind having me live with you."

"All your stuff's in your car right now?" Jaime asked in surprise.

"What's not in your closet, yeah." Oliver nodded.

"*Our* closet," Jaime corrected happily. "Let's go bring it in." He rose to his feet and pulled Oliver up with him.

"We could do that. Or..."

He stilled and looked at Oliver. "Or?"

"Or I can call in for a day off tomorrow and we can do something else tonight?" Oliver's cheeks reddened as he spoke, and Jaime hoped he never lost his bashfulness.

"The day off won't be an issue." Jaime curled his arms around Oliver's waist. "I have an in with the boss." He planted his hands on Oliver's butt and kneaded it. "What do you have in mind to fill our time instead?"

Oliver reached behind him, took Jaime's hand off his butt, and linked their fingers together. "Come with me to *our* bedroom and I'll show you."

The End

About the Author

Cardeno C.—CC to friends—is a hopeless romantic who wants to add a lot of happiness and a few awwws into a reader's day. Writing is a nice break from real life as a corporate type and volunteer work with gay rights organizations. Cardeno's stories range from sweet to intense, contemporary to paranormal, long to short, but they always include strong relationships and walks into the happily-ever-after sunset.

Email:

cardenoc@gmail.com

Website:

www.cardenoc.com

Twitter:

twitter.com/cardenoc

Facebook:

facebook.com/CardenoC

Pinterest:

pinterest.com/cardenoC

Blog:

caferisque.blogspot.com

Other Books by Cardeno C.

FRIENDS
Not a Game

SIPHON
Johnnie

HOPE
McFarland's Farm
Jesse's Diner

PACK
Blue Mountain
Red River

NOVELS
Strange Bedfellows
Perfect Imperfections

MATES
In Your Eyes
Until Forever Comes
Wake Me Up Inside

FAMILY
The Half of Us
Something in the Way He Needs
Strong Enough
More Than Everything

HOME

He Completes Me

Home Again

Just What the Truth Is

Love at First Sight

The One Who Saves Me

Where He Ends and I Begin

Walk With Me

NOVELLAS

A Shot at Forgiveness

All of Me

Places in Time

In Another Life & Eight Days

Jumping In

Available Now

Perfect Imperfections

Accountant slash bartender Reg will show rock star Jeremy how to have fun…and possibly fall in love.

Hollywood royalty Jeremy Jameson has lived a sheltered life with music as his sole focus and only friend. Before embarking on yet another international concert tour, he wanders into a bar in what he considers the middle-of-nowhere and meets a man who wins him over with his friendly smile and easy-going nature. Accountant slash bartender slash adventure-seeker Reg Moore has fun talking and drinking with The Jeremy Jameson and can't say no when the supposedly straight rock star makes him a once in a lifetime offer: keep him company on his tour by playing the part of his boyfriend.

Listening to music, traveling the world, and jumping off cliffs is fun. Falling in love is even better. But to stay with Jeremy after the stage lights dim, Reg will need to help him realize there's nothing pretend about their relationship.

Strange Bedfellows

Can the billionaire son of a Democratic president build a family with the congressman son of a Republican senator? Forget politics, love makes strange bedfellows.

As the sole offspring of the Democratic United States president and his political operative wife, Trevor Moga was raised in an environment driven by the election cycle. During childhood, he fantasized about living in a made-for-television family, and as an adult, he rejected all things politics and built a highly successful career as far from his parents as possible.

Newly elected congressman Ford Hollingsworth is Republican royalty. The grandson of a revered governor and son of a respected senator, he was bred to value faith, family, and the goal of seeing a Hollingsworth in the White House.

When Trevor and Ford meet, sparks fly and a strong friendship is formed. But can the billionaire son of a Democratic president build a family with the congressman son of a Republican senator? Forget politics, love makes strange bedfellows.

The Half of Us
(A Family Story)

If short-tempered Jason can open his heart and life to optimistic Abe, he might finally find the family he craves.

Short-tempered, arrogant heart surgeon Jason Garcia grew up wanting a close-knit family, but believes he ruined those dreams when he broke up his marriage. The benefit of divorce is having as much random sex as he wants, and it's a benefit Jason is exploiting when he meets a sweet, shy man at a bar and convinces him to go home for a no-strings-attached night of fun.

Eight years living in Las Vegas hasn't dimmed Abe Green's optimism, earnestness, or desire to find the one. When a sexy man with lonely eyes propositions him, Abe decides to give himself a birthday present—one night of spontaneous fun with no thoughts of the future. But one night turns into two and then three, and Abe realizes his heart is involved.

For the first time, Abe feels safe enough with someone he respects and adores to let go of his inhibitions in the bedroom. If Jason can get past his own inhibitions and open his heart and his life to Abe, he might finally find the family he craves.

Strong Enough
(A Family Story)

When a casual hookup turns into the potential for love, staid Spencer realizes he wants to build a life with vibrant Emilio.

When twenty-two-year-old Emilio Sanchez sees handsome Spencer Derdinger walking by his construction site, Emilio makes it his goal to seduce the shy professor. Getting Spencer into bed isn't difficult, but Emilio soon learns that earning the trust of a man deeply hurt will take time and patience. With a prize like brilliant, sweet Spencer on the line, Emilio decides he is strong enough to face the challenge.

Spencer is surprised when he's approached by the gorgeous construction worker he's admired from the safety of his office window. Acting spontaneously for the first time in his thirty-eight years, Spencer takes Emilio home. When the casual hookup turns into the potential for love, Spencer realizes that if he wants to build a life with Emilio, he'll need to be strong enough to slay his personal demons and learn to trust again.

Walk With Me
(A Home Story)

Serious, responsible Seth longs for sexy, outspoken Eli but must decide if he's willing to veer from his safe life-plan.

When Eli Block steps into his parents' living room and sees his childhood crush sitting on the couch, he starts a shameless campaign to seduce the young rabbi. Unfortunately, Seth Cohen barely remembers Eli and he resolutely shuts down all his advances. As a tenuous and then binding friendship forms between the two men, Eli must find a way to move past his unrequited love while still keeping his best friend in his life. Not an easy feat when the same person occupies both roles.

Professional, proper Seth is shocked by Eli's brashness, overt sexuality, and easy defiance of societal norms. But he's also drawn to the happy, funny, light-filled man. As their friendship deepens over the years, Seth watches Eli mature into a man he admires and respects. When Seth finds himself longing for what Eli had so easily offered, he has to decide whether he's willing to veer from his safe life-plan to build a future with Eli.

Just What the Truth Is
(A Home Story)

If Ben wants to find love with Micah, he'll have to own up to the truth of who he is.

People-pleaser Ben Forman has been in the closet so long he has almost convinced himself he is straight, but his denial train gets derailed when hotshot lawyer Micah Trains walks into his life. Micah is brilliant, funny, driven…and he assumes Ben is gay and starts dating him. Finding himself truly happy for the first time, Ben doesn't have the willpower to resist Micah's affection.

When his relationship with Micah heats up, Ben realizes has a problem: his parents won't tolerate a gay son and self-confident Micah isn't the type to hide. If Ben wants to maintain his hold on his happiness, he'll have to decide what's important and own up to the truth of who he is. The trouble is figuring out just what that truth is.